From Mukherji
To Malhotra

The story of two amazing women extremely unlike each other…

Published by

Office: A-42, Dayanand Colony,

New Delhi(South)-110024

Emails: ganivpanjrath@yahoo.co.in, tannaazirani@gmail.com

ISBN-13: 978-81-949782-4-4
ISBN 10: 81-949782-4-6

MRP: $15/-

Book size: 5.5*8.5

Printed and bound by Creative Crows Publishers LLP

Contents

My daughter has turned 14 and I ask her, “How does it feel?”

“I feel ancient – so old!”

“Really? So how do you think I feel…And Papa…?”

“Oh God, you guys are Neanderthals!” came the reply, with that bored look and eyeroll so typical of teens that is uniform across the world! Something of a smirk, cracking a smart one and yet pretending not to laugh! A shrug of those bony shoulders, trying ever so hard to look older, ending up with a snort and a giggle!

I want to smack her bottom and tell her to get lost! And then…

“Do you know that at 14, your grandmother was already married?”

“No!” (Some reaction there – Horror! Shock!!)

“How could she be? She was too young. Did she not go to school or college?”

***

BOOK I

1

Let's Begin...

Narsingharh is a princely state of Madhya Pradesh. From the internet one learns trivia like the erstwhile Parmar Maharaja had a privy purse of Rs1,15,000/ in the year 1948, before Indira Gandhi decided to ban privy purses, that is.

The amount of money may appear a trifle compared to today's salaries and bank deposits of politicians and businessmen – the maharajas of today!

But, back in 1917, when Dr Manmatha Nath Mukherji was a doctor in the Royal Court of the then Maharaja, life was opulent, to say the least! There was a motor vehicle to transport him and his family to the court, and on other outings, especially with the royal family. Incidentally, that was only the second motor vehicle in the state, next only to the one owned by the Maharaja.

There were reputed to be 1,025 cars in Bombay in 1910. Even then, motor cars were a rarity, especially in far flung places like this small rural town with its own Raja! And if you happened to be in close affinity to the 'royal' family, some of the airs and graces did rub off on you.

The good doctor was married young as was the tradition in those days. In early 1908, very shortly after his graduation from the Calcutta Medical College, he was married to Mrinalini Debi who came from a semi royal family herself;

and like other girls from her stratum of society, she had been home schooled, and was very comfortable reading and writing Bangla and English, and knew all her Math – such that she could actually do complicated everyday problems with alacrity.

The Maharaja of Narsinghgarh was a young man then and liked the earnest energy and learning capability of the doctor. Being quite the anglophile himself, he sent the young doctor to England for a refresher course. His specific injunction was that Dr Mukherji should know all there was to know about medical help for women and children, especially girls.

When Dr Mukherji returned from England after a six-month refresher course, the couple was given a lovely little English style cottage with four bedrooms, a large kitchen, a well laid out garden with flowerbeds, potted plants and a manicured lawn. At the back was a well-tended kitchen garden which provided all the vegetables one could need. Mrinalini Debi had enough people to look after the garden; in fact, the gardeners who looked after the royal gardens were ordered to look after the garden of the doctor. They were happy to do so as '*daktarni*' was a very gentle soul with a very large heart. She always gave the workers their morning tea with a sweet and a savoury which she made sure was given in her presence. She believed that the workers should be looked after and she had no *purdah* from any of them. "They are like my own children," she would maintain.

Over the next six years, two boys and one girl were added to the Mukherji family. In 1917, Kadambini was born, the fourth child and the second daughter. At a later stage, three more boys and two more girls were born, a right round figure of nine – four girls and five boys!

A teacher had been ordered to start the lessons for all the kids. The school room had the boys sitting down on the floor and learning Sanskrit from Panditji, and English and Maths from Mr Joseph. At a later stage they were to join the other boys of the royal family, to write the 'matric' exam.

The girls were taught in *purdah* (a curtain behind which the ladies had to remain). A thin muslin *purdah* was put up in the same room as the boys. The girls sat on the other side of the *purdah* and learnt all there was to learn from the masters. Dr Mukherji was very sure that his girls would learn all that the boys would. Maybe higher studies too, if any one of his girls showed any exceptional promise.

Very soon, it was time to send out the boys for higher studies. The eldest son was sent to college in Jhansi. The eldest daughter was married at the age of 12 to another medical student who was almost 15 years older than her.

By 1931, it was also Kadambini's time to get married.

***

2

The Banerji 'Khandan' of Gwalior

If you have ever walked through the old bustling city of Gwalior and stopped to stare at a crumbling road sign that said **Banerji Galli,** then know, that you are looking at the last remaining landmark of the Banerji clan that lived in the old city of Gwalior, at the turn of the century.

Tejeshwar Nath Banerji was a well-established contractor who ran a very large household, in keeping with his affluent status. He had his sisters and brothers and fourteen children of his own to bring up. Legend has it that, at one time, food for a hundred people was cooked daily!

But that is neither here nor there, our story is concerned with negotiations for a marriage!

So, when the feelers went out for TN Banerji's promising young son, Nobin, who was tall and good looking, a good student and a great athlete, seeking to marry Dr Manmatha Nath Mukherji's second daughter, Kadambini, there was really no cause to refuse. Ray *babu,* the family jeweller for the Banerjis was very happy when his suggestion was accepted – yes!

Those days the family jewellers or the family barbers were also the marriage brokers. They did not charge a fee but they made a place for themselves in the families' good books. Of course, among the many gifts ordained for the guests and family members, the brokers were also given silks and money.

One has to remember, that Narsingharh was barely 350 kms away from the larger kingdom of Gwalior; and although the royal families were not poor, in what we know of poor, they were not extraordinarily rich either. There was always jewellery to remodel and recycle. Thus, Manik Babu and Ray Babu had free access to the more affluent households of the two cities. The Banerjis had money while the Mukherjis were semi royalty!

Those were the days of a different kind of networking!

No social media, no telephones, no information about the bride or bridegroom, except what the middlemen had to say. The bride and groom saw each other for the first time only on their wedding day.

3

The Preparations and The Biye (Wedding)

So, now the day of Kadambini's wedding dawned!

On one wall of my mother's Puja room is a photograph of my mother on her wedding day. She is dark with a round face, wearing a then fashionable lace trimmed blouse and a sari – never could make out the details. I guess it was a Banarasi – those were the wedding saris of yesteryear.

What does it feel like to be 14 and on the verge of getting married?

In accordance with the parents' diktats, Kadambini had been groomed for marriage from childhood. There was no question of competing with the boys or seeking higher education, however much the good doctor may have wanted them to. The final verdict was Mrinalini Debi's – namely, that when it is time to get married, there has to be no objection, whatsoever! Education or otherwise; no Mukherji daughter was going to college for higher studies. Thus, it was settled.

Did the boy and girl meet each other? Did they talk to each other?

No. That was not done – the verdict of the broker was understood to be the last word. It was up to him to inform the concerned parties if there were any skeletons in the respective cupboards. It would be the broker's job to inform the other party if the girl had a limp or was cross-eyed or had any such 'defect'. So, the humiliation of rejection could be avoided. Those were the ways of the genteel.

Kadambini in her own words has this to say of her wedding day:

"I was so nervous and anxious. I had to fast all day, which was not really a problem for me. But my stomach! How many times I had to run to the toilet! I actually lost count; until Baba intervened and ordered some barley water for me to control the loose motions! He was worried I would collapse at the time of the wedding! Ma was very keen on following the rules scrupulously and she was quite sure that nothing would happen to me if I stayed on an empty stomach until the wedding was done! But Baba was not sure and he did not want any mishaps – hence the barley water with *mishri* and lime juice!

"It certainly saved the day!

"As a rule, I had very little problems with my stomach because we had regular cleansing with castor oil (one teaspoonful once a week! Ugh!!), so, all of us brothers and sisters had pretty strong stomachs. It must have been the overeating at the *Aiburo bhaat*, (the yesteryear equivalent of today's bachelorette party) two days earlier combined with my anxiety. Every one of my *Mashis*, (mother's sister) *Pishis* (Father's sister) and *Kakimas* (Father's brothers' wives), aunts of various degrees, was stuffing food down my throat and I was not supposed to say no to any of these 'loving' ministrations!

"That is the only reason for my stomach to give way, so I believed.

"Many years later I learnt that the stomach could give way with an overdose of anxiety too!

"A lot of hectic activity was going on in the outer verandah. Other than '*alpana*' (rangolis) done by the women, *'mangal ghats'* (clay vessels that hold mango leaves and a coconut on top), were being placed in the four corners of the house. At the spot, a swastika was drawn in vermilion, before the ghat was placed on it. These clay vessels are used to ward off evil spirits and usher in good fortune, in unison with a garland of mango leaves. The entrance of the bride's home usually sports a copper version of the *mangal ghat.*"

From my mother's enormous cupboard, I had extracted a gorgeously light tissue sari, with gold bootis (Motifs) and thin gold borders. I had asked Ma, "Is this your wedding sari?" She had smiled and said, "Na go, your dadu wore this as a safa (Turban). After the wedding I was given this to wear as a sari and to keep it safe. It was a token from my father to remind me that I must now be responsible to protect my father's dignity and name and that I should never do anything to sully his reputation."

My daughter now took it from me, held it against her and I could see her visualizing the scenario. Very tentatively she asked me if she could keep it. Then she quickly changed her mind. "You keep it for now. I will take it when I can be responsible enough to look after it."

Kadambini told me over the years: "The *borjatri* (the wedding procession of the groom) was coming and there was a lot of excitement. Didi and I could see the procession; and then Didi pointed out Baba – '*Ayee! Baba ke dekhe chish?*' (hey have you seen Baba?) He looks so good with his *safa* and that gold clip given by Raja Sahib…And there is your future husband!!'

"I hid my face in my veil – I was so nervous and embarrassed. These words I learnt much later – then it was only '*lojja*'!! (embarrassment)

"Some more '*lojja*' was to be removed at the next stage of the wedding!

"I was carried on a *piri*, (a small flat wooden seat), by my brothers and male cousins. I had my face covered behind *paan* (betel leaf) leaves. Once I came face to face with your father, I was supposed to let him see me while I was told to take a look at him. This was the first time we were actually seeing each other; and, while everyone was laughing and enjoying themselves with snide remarks, I was dying of *lojja*. This was called the *shubho drishti*. All the women were doing ulu – strange yodeling sounds which I now know, date back to very primitive times. Ululating sounds are used to ward off evil spirits. Along with the ulu, the *shankh* (conch) was also being blown to welcome a new beginning.

"Although everything is a haze after that, I do know we exchanged garlands before sitting down with the priest, for the serious part of the wedding. At the *bashor jagai*, (a tradition where the young couple are kept awake all night on their wedding night) that night, my brothers and sisters, cousins, aunts and uncles kept us awake all night. Since the wedding was not yet complete, the couple had to be kept awake and not allowed to be on their own. The next day was the last part of the wedding in Baba's house.

"I was crying copious tears as I knew that I was saying goodbye to my childhood, away from Baba and Ma and my favourite garden. Soon it was time to go.

"Raja sahib had given us his Rolls Royce to drive down to Gwalior to your Baba's home, my new *shoshur bari!*" (The home of the in laws!)

***

4

The Banerji Home

Inside a huge vintage wooden door, with lethal metal studs and spikes which one normally finds in fortresses, the courtyard opened out into many rooms around a large spacious open area. There were rooms and rooms and more rooms.

In the centre of the courtyard was a *tulsi* plant in a large pot with a burning lamp. The moment Kadambini stepped inside the doorway, the conch shells were called out in unison and in sequence. All the elder married women of the family were standing in a line to blow the conch shells – quite a royal sound and also quite a sight!

Colourful *Benarasi* saris and heaped *sindoor* (red colour applied by a married woman) in the partings of the hair with feet and hands covered in *alta* designs, that is, a red liquid applied on hands and feet, made for a really colourful sight. Kadambini was asked to step into a *thaala* (large platter) which had red coloured water in it. She was told it was diluted *alta.* She was told to put out her right foot first while entering the verandah. She left very dainty red footprints as she walked into the house.

In a total contrast to this colourful show, from behind the iron slats of one large room, peeped out gray faces of the widows. Old worn-out white saris now turned to a dull gray, no other vestments, no blouses and no jewellery.

They had been told to stay in the room, as widows were not allowed to be present to greet the new bride. They were considered *manhoos, omongol,* that is, inauspicious, in any language. It was a cruel system in tandem with the widows wearing white saris, with shorn hair and no adornments of any kind.

Banerji Babu would not have given in to this cruel system; as he loved and respected his sisters, Bimala and Basanti, his widowed *Bhabhi* (sister-in-law) Satyavati, and his lone widowed daughter Charulata, who was actually a child widow. Yet he could not stand up against the stringent diktats of Bangla Brahmin society. He had kept these four women at home and had tolerated the snide remarks from other Bengalis of the city.

According to the elders of the Bangla society, the widows should have been living in Brindavan or Mathura or Varanasi with other widows, sharing a frugal living space.

Every time there was a wedding or *upanayana* – the thread ceremony of a Brahmin boy coming of age – at home, Banerji Babu would have to leave these women inside their room, where they slept on the floor with no mattresses or pillows. The big window compensated for their being apart; at least they could see what was going on.

But the *purut moshai* (the pujari/priest) was not happy about this particular arrangement either, as he did not want a glimpse of their faces; he believed, that even their *chhaya* or shadow would be *oshubh!* But the patriarch would have none of it!

The ceremonies for the welcome of the new bride carried on with the *shankh* and the *ulu* while Kadambini was led into her room which had a large four poster bed all decorated with flowers. In the evening was the *bou bhat* where the new bride would serve food to all the elders of the house as well as the guests.

Everyone would sit on the floor, cross legged, while the leaf plates were laid out and then the servings began. There is a very specific order which is always meticulously followed. It starts with the salt, then the pickle, the rice, the *bhajas* (fries), the dal, the fish curry, and then the chutney or the *ombol* – a kind of finger licking sweet-sour tangy concoction that is served at the end, just before the sweet!

The dessert is always awaited with great joy – *roshogulla, kaala jam, payash!* What a treat!

There were at least seventy-five to eighty people and poor Kadambini was told that she would be serving the rice to all the venerated elders of the family, maybe thirty people. The others would be served by the other members of the family. Her husband was also helping serve the food.

Once Nobin and Kadambini knocked into each other while serving the food. All the folks sitting around started laughing out loud.

"*Ayee Nobin, Bouma ke shahajjo kor!* (help our new bride) *Bechara!* She can't carry all that rice by herself!"

More laughter…

Kadambini covered her face 'cos she knew she was blushing!

That night was *phool shojja* or the bed of flowers – commonly known as the wedding night where the wedding was to be consummated.

Both Nobin and Kadambini were virgins – whatever they had to do and learn, it had to be instinctive with no prior information or knowledge.

Many years later, Ma told me when I was on the verge of getting married, "Your Baba and I spoke at length and he was very gentle and kind. He had read a whole lot of books and knew about the shyness and virginity of the Indian women and how penetration would be very painful. He told me all about it. Now when I think back, maybe my mother should have told me; but then, back in those days, mothers and daughters never spoke... especially about sex and personal issues."

I told her that the school had explained these things to us way back when we were in the 8th and 9th standards. She was quite taken aback because she did not know that I knew something about the birds and the bees!

5

Life Goes On

That petite 14-year-old became a mother, six months after she turned 15. Kadambini went to her parents in Narsingharh, where the infant girl was born amid celebrations and great joy. Nobin arrived on time for the celebrations with good news of his own. He was joining St John's College at Agra as he had been given a sports scholarship and was planning to study Law. His father had passed away by now, and the other elders at home did not want him to study further.

He went on to Agra where he carried on playing football and hockey and some occasional tennis. Yet he scored well in all his tests. This was also the time when he developed a kinship with the Srivastava family of Agra.

On his little round table, next to Baba's cupboard, were all his medicines, his hair oil, his combs hairbrushes and other toiletries. In the midst of all this was a vintage photograph of an elderly gentleman in a suit and tie.

I asked him, "Who is he? your grandfather?"

Very lovingly he picked up the photograph, wiped it with his hand and told me, "My father passed away when I had decided to pursue the study of law. This gentleman, Babuji, became my surrogate father; he gave me a home and he gave me a direction – thanks to him I am a lawyer. After my Baba's passing, I knew I had to get out of Gwalior: If I had to make something of myself, I had to leave home because all the elders of the family were against higher education.

"I found a whole new set of brothers and sisters in Babuji's home. Raghu the second son and I became buddies because both of us were in the University hockey team.

"There was a profound atmosphere in the house – all the boys were hard working and excelled in school. They were also good in sports, which made for a healthy combination. While I became a lawyer, all the Srivastava boys became government officers – and the sisters were married to Professors and other senior officers.

"When I first heard the rumors of a 'swayamvar' for the eldest Srivastava daughter Uma didi, I was awestruck. I was told that a number of officers had been invited. I had thought that particular event was for royalty only.

"This event was not as extravagant as the ones referred to in the tales of the Ramayana and Ayodhya. But then, it was grand, at least to my inexperienced eyes! Besides, the family could afford a lavish event like this; and one Ram Prasad did make the cut – another officer who was Raghu's senior and then currently posted in Delhi.

"The wedding was extravagant, in keeping with Babuji's status."

Baba smiled and his eyes twinkled,

"Your mother was also there with your eldest sister and brother. This was also the time when my initiation into the nitty gritty of the law began when I became a 'junior' to Barrister J C Chakravarthy, a legal luminary of Agra.

6

The Move to Meerut – Another Phase Begins

It was the year when the first rumblings of an international conflict were heard.1937 saw a full-scale war between Japan and China. In 1939 Hitler marched into Poland, annexed Belgium and began consolidating his empire. No one had imagined a conflict of this scale when World War II started.

By then, Nobin was ready to start his own personal war – of ambition and grit.

One day Babuji summoned Nobin for a talk.

In a frail voice, he said, "Nobin, you have done your share of internship. To my mind I feel that you are ready to start your own independent journey. I want you to move to Meerut where my dear friend, Raja Ram Mithal, an eminent lawyer, is looking for a sharp young lad to work with him."

Nobin was sad that Babuji was sending him away and he did not want to go far away from his foster father.

"Babuji, why can't I practice independently from here? I am happy here – and I dread going to a new place where I will know no one."

"No Nobin, my time is up. You will not be able to concentrate on your work unless you have a dedicated lawyer to guide you. I know Raja Ram will look after you and will guide you on the right path."

Nobin was crying. He touched Babuji's feet and left.

Babuji passed away, soon after.

Nobin moved to Meerut where a whole new world waited for him. Raghu gave Nobin his car and driver to move the family to Meerut. They found a small two room house in the locality called Khairnagar, in old Meerut city. It was located in a congested locality where houses were built cheek by jowl, a typical *'mohalla'* where everyone knew everyone else. And when a good looking, obviously educated young man comes into the locality, with a wife and four small children, it is a matter of curiosity, no doubt. Lots of windows and doors were opened, ostensibly to let in air. But then, one had to see who was moving into the neighbourhood!

On the first day itself, Mrs Mishra came over to check out Kadambini and the kids while Nobin went to meet Mithal saab, his new mentor.

Kadambini had hardly interacted with outsiders and knew very little Hindi. All that she did know, was, courtesy the Srivastava family. But when Mrs Mishra knocked on the door, she opened it to greet the elderly lady.

"Namaste *behen.*"

"Namaste! Please come in."

Mrs Mishra stepped in and was astounded by the number of trunks inside the house.

"Itna samaan? Kahan rakhoge?"

Kadambini was a little taken aback. She did not know how to tell the lady that her entire household was in those trunks and as soon as she was able to put things in their place, the trunks would 'disappear'.

She smiled and said nothing.

Then Mrs Mishra said, *"Bacchon ke liye doodh chahiye?"*

That Kadambini understood and nodded her head vigorously, yes yes!

Mrs Mishra went away a wee bit disgruntled, after promising to send the doodhwala (milkman) the next morning. She was disappointed as she had been expecting a nice gossipy chatty morning! But if the young woman could not speak, at least not in Hindi, then what was the point in wasting time with her?

She stopped at the next door to chat with her old friend Manju and gave her the lowdown on Kadambini. *"Bangalan hai, Hindi bolna nahin aata. Kaise rahegi yahan? Pata nahin."*

The last with a ponderous shaking of the head!

But Kadambini made a home with ease and comfort. The children were put into decent schools: Indrajeet the first boy, was enrolled in Nanakchand High School while the three girls were enrolled in Durgabari Anglo Bengali Girls' school where the new Bengali family was welcomed with open arms.

The years rolled on. Gaurav, the second son was welcomed with great joy and then two years later Probir the third son arrived.

Kadambini trusted her husband to build her a home big enough to accommodate her growing brood of children. She was a great home maker, a *grahini*, who made sure to provide good healthy food. She was also strong in her beliefs that her children needed good education, boys and girls alike. There had to be sports and music also. In the cramped gullies of old Meerut city, there were no facilities for sports of any kind.

In the midst of it all, Kadambini enrolled for her Intermediate exam from Raghunath Girls' College. She was allowed to appear privately for her exams. She was a voracious reader and she read everything from the Readers' Digest (her husband and daughters' favourite) to Shakespeare's plays, to the Bengali magazine called *'Sondesh'* which came by post from Kolkata. But she could not get her tongue around Hindi and still found it difficult to speak. The girls laughed at her Hindi, but she took it in good grace!

The family moved into Nandan Garden, a sprawling bungalow which belonged to Raghu Srivastav's family. It was rented to Kamdambini's family for a small sum. Right next door, was another sprawling bungalow which came up for sale a few years later. Kadambini had been putting aside small sums of money to invest in a home of her own, a place where she could do the gardening and entertaining, as her mother had done. She was also keen to have more space as she was adding more kids to her brood.

Nobin was developing quite a reputation for his sincerity and hard work. His clients came from far and wide, searching for this earnest young man. His hard work paid off and little luxuries were added regularly.

One of the first ones was a car! They bought a second hand *Landmaster*, the precursor of the later day *Ambassador.* That was India's first indigenous car which rolled out from the factory in Kolkata.

7

World War II and its Impact

The great world war was raging. Indian troops were involved in various spots, fighting alongside the British troops under the flag of the Queen. From 1939 to 1945, two and a half million Indian troops fought in different sectors as far apart as the China Burma sector and the North Africa sector.

Indians fought with distinction throughout the world, including in the European theatre against Germany, in North Africa against Germany and Italy, in the South Asian region defending India against the Japanese and fighting the Japanese in Burma. Indians also aided in liberating British colonies such as Singapore and Hong Kong after the Japanese surrender in August 1945. Over 87,000 Indian soldiers (including those from modern day Pakistan, Nepal, and Bangladesh) died in World War II. Field Marshal Sir Claude Auchinleck, Commander-in-Chief of the Indian Army from 1942 asserted the British "...couldn't have come through both wars World War I and World War II if they hadn't had the Indian Army."

In all the hype of winning the wars in different sectors a small news item was neglected by the British. For the first (and probably the last!) time in the history of India, a man-made famine in Bengal wiped out millions between the years 1943-44. After all these years of secrecy, it has finally been revealed that the then Prime Minister of Great Britain, Winston

Churchill, who was notorious for his racist beliefs, is said to have diverted the rice and other provisions away from Bengal to other more pressing needs of the realm!

Be that as it may, the deaths of nearly three million Bengalis left a deep impact on those Bengali families who were away from Bengal – the *probashi* Bengalis. To keep the Bengali spirit alive, *probashi* families grew and it was quite common to hear of seven, eight or ten kids in a family.

Yet they maintained their culture and their refined tastes. Music had to be listened to and also learnt; music was a regular fixture in most Bengali households along with a few musical instruments like the *sitar*, *tanpura*, or the *tabla*.

8

Kali

The store room and its massive trunks that housed all the family woolens was a great place to dive into and pull out 'interesting stuff'. One of the larger trunks was deep enough for me to get in and stand straight. I could probably be locked inside too! But there were more interesting things to do. I discovered a brown woolen tweed coat with very smart brass buttons. It was cut in the fashion of the old great coats worn by soldiers, but it was smaller in size. I pulled it out and put it on in front of the mirror in the bedroom. I thought I looked very smart with the old black pants and my school shoes.

Ma came looking for me – something I was supposed to do and obviously I had not done. She walked in and stopped.

She suddenly went very still. Very softly and gently told me, "Do not wear this. Put it back in the trunk."

She turned around and went away – something was very wrong. Was Ma crying?

Then my Mejdi (second sister) came and took off the coat and folded it up. I volunteered to open the trunk and put it back inside.

My curiosity remained. A few weeks later we were sitting around together, and the topic came up again. Then I was told the truth of the coat. Both Sejdi (third sister) and Mejdi sat us younger ones down and told us.

Tragedy strikes

Indrajeet was the best possible son one could imagine: Though I never met him or saw him – I realize there are no pictures of him anywhere in the house.

"Indrajeet was the darling of all who knew him," Mejdi and Sejdi took turns in telling me the story.

"He was tall, good looking and very polite. He had a great way with him and he could talk to all the uncles and aunts. In fact, he was comfortable talking to all the elderly English who frequented Alexander Club and wanted to guide him for his tennis lessons. He was a great sportsman, and like Baba, excelled in anything he chose to play.

"He was also learning music and could sing well too, in spite of the fact that his voice was just getting over the 'cracking' phase of teenage. Ma and Baba both adored him. And then one day he came back, feverish after his tennis session at the Club.

"When the fever did not break after all of Ma's homely ministrations, the doctors were called in. And they came by the dozen – apparently, they could not identify what had caused the malaise. The doctors tried all they could but to no avail.

"He kept asking Ma for a mango to eat and since the doctors had forbidden, she could not give him one.

"He worried that it was his birthday a few days later, 'bhalo hoye jaa botoh Ma?' (I will be okay by then, won't I?)

"He died two days later."

Mejdi and Sejdi were both sobbing now!

Sejdi added, "For many years afterwards, Ma never ate mangoes. She would break down every time she even saw a mango. And she never celebrated the birthdays of any of the kids ever again."

Indrajeet was short of his 14th birthday when he passed on.

From Baba I learned that Ma had quite lost her mental balance after the death of her first-born son.

"I took her to various doctors, astrologers, pujaris – wherever she wanted to go," said Baba. "Finally, when we reached Dakshineshwar and my cousin, who lived there, took her to the temple, she calmed down. She got her diksha, (initiation into the ritual of prayers) with the promise of daily prayers to Ma Kali and a daily Sandhya arati. She came back to Meerut, more like her old self. It took a whole year and a few months for things to get back to normal – her puja helped.

"She started meeting people and attending the social functions where we were invited. She found peace in her prayers. For all of you kids, it was also good to have prayers done every day at home. Then your Ma began going to the Kalibari on all Saturdays."

The Kalibari

Kali is the Hindu goddess (or Devi) of death, time, and doomsday; and is often associated with sexuality and violence. She is also considered a strong mother-figure and symbolic of motherly love. Kali also embodies *shakti* – feminine energy, creativity and fertility – and is an incarnation of Parvati, wife of the great Hindu god Shiva. She is most often represented in art as a fearful fighting figure with a necklace of heads, skirt of arms, lolling tongue, and brandishing a knife dripping with blood.

Kali's name derives from the Sanskrit meaning 'she who is black' or 'she who is death', but she is also known as Chaturbhuja Kali, Chinnamastā, or Kaushika. As an embodiment of time Kali devours all things: she is irresistibly attractive to mortals and gods, and can also represent (particularly in later traditions) the benevolence of a mother goddess.

The goddess is particularly worshipped in eastern and southern India and specifically in Assam, Kerala, Kashmir, and Bengal, where she is now worshipped in the yearly festival of Kali Puja held on the night of a new moon, and in the Kalighat Temple in the city of Calcutta.

Kali's Birth:

There are several traditions of how Kali came into existence. One version relates that when the warrior goddess Durga, who had ten arms each carrying a weapon and who rode a lion or tiger in battle, fought with Mahishasura (or Mahisa), the buffalo demon, she became so enraged that she turned black with anger and took on the form of Kali. Once born, the black goddess went wild and ate all the demons she came across, stringing their heads on a chain which she wore around her neck. It seemed impossible to calm Kali's bloody attacks, which now extended to any wrongdoers; and both people and gods were at a loss as to what to do! Fortunately, the mighty Shiva stopped Kali's destructive rampage by lying down in her path, and when the goddess realised just who she was standing on, she finally calmed down. From this story is explained Kali's association with battlegrounds and areas where cremation is carried out.

Kali & Raktabija : In yet another version of Kali's birth, there is the story of the terrible demon Raktabija (Blood-seed). This demon was, like most demons, causing a great deal of trouble with people and gods alike; but even worse, was his ability to produce more demons every time a drop of his blood spilt to the ground. Therefore, each time Raktabija was attacked, the only result was more demons to deal with. The gods decided to work together and combine all of their *shakti* or divine energy and produce one super being that could destroy Raktabija; the result was Kali.

Given all the divine weapons of the gods, Kali swiftly sought out Raktabija and his demons and proceeded to swallow them all whole so as not to spill anymore blood in the process. Raktabija himself was killed when Kali lopped off his head with a sword and then drank all of his blood, making sure none fell to the ground and thereby ensuring no more demons could menace the world.

*Extracts from Mark Cartwright (Cartwright, M. 2013, June 21). **Kali**. Ancient History Encyclopedia. Retrieved from https://www.ancient.eu/Kali.*

What Mark Cartwright with his western sensibilities does not know and understand is, that the 'lolling tongue' which he connects to her blood thirsty rampage of killing the demons, came out when she stepped on her husband, Shiva. It would have been the equivalent of today's 'oops!'

A Hindu woman, leave alone a Goddess, can never dream of stepping on her husband. Yet Shiva had little choice. Brahma, the Creator asked Shiva to intervene or else the entire universe would be destroyed. Shiva knew the path Kali would take so he silently lay down in her path. The moment she stepped on him; her anger dissipated. She cooled down and stood stock still.

These were the inputs my Ma had given me – part of the many small stories she told us!

The Kalibari in Meerut was located in a narrow alleyway in the *sadar bazaar* locality of Meerut Cantonment. Meerut was an old military base, considered very crucial since it was close to Delhi. Within a triangle, connected with narrow lanes, was a *gurdwara* and a mosque. If one was to trace back the origins of all the three, the reason for their unique presence here would be obvious. They were meant to cater to the Indian soldiers – Hindus, Muslims and Sikhs – who made up the British Indian army. There were enough churches in the vicinity of the regimental stations, but these places were a little far away. Yet all three together!

When I learnt to drive and got my official license, one of the first things Baba did was to entrust me with driving Ma to the Kalibari every Saturday.

Inside the Kalibari

Ma had told us how some of the earliest Kalibaris used to have human sacrifice as decreed by the tantrics of yesteryear. Earlier, as a young preteen with my heightened sensibilities, I was a little scared of entering the place. I followed Ma with trepidation, half expecting blood spattered entrails all over the place. But the place was clean.

On the way back, I did ask Ma about the sacrifices. She told me, "When this 'purut moshai' (the priest/pujari) took over the temple he stopped all sacrifices. He pledged 101 drops of his own blood so that no sacrifice ever took place again."

When I saw him, I was amazed – he was a tall, strapping and well-built man, who always wore a dhoti, come winter, summer or rain! As the years went by, sometimes I would see a shawl on his shoulders, especially during the winters.

When I started driving Ma to the temple, I would do the pushpanjali (prayers said with flowers) with her, with my eyes shut, all religious fervour, with the firm belief that any less would take away from the sincerity of my prayer. Then one day when I knelt down to do the last bit of prayer, I noticed that the goddess was standing on the chest of a blue person. On the way home, I asked Ma what was the significance of the whole scenario. That is when my kid sister and I heard the story of how Shiva lay on the ground because he knew that that was the only way that Kali could be stopped.

The temple was always crowded, not so much from worshippers as from extended family. The family that looked after the temple, starting with the purut moshai, his wife, half a dozen kids, his sisters and their kids and so on! Everyone lived on the proceeds of the temple. The younger kids of the family started going to school when my mother insisted that they should – she had always been a great promoter of education for all.

9

St Mary's Academy

The Patrician Brothers from Ireland set up their first co-ed school in Meerut, called St Mary's Academy, in the year 1952. It had begun as an all-boys' school. It had come into being, right in time for Gaurav, the older of the Banerji boys to be the first enrolment; Probir, the second son joined the next year. The British had recently left; and all progressive Indian parents felt that an English education was the right thing, especially for their boys.

The three older girls were enrolled in Durga Bari Anglo Bengali School, where they learnt Bengali, English, Mathematics and the Sciences. Then came along another five girls; of these, the four younger girls were admitted to St Mary's, while the solitary sister who had the misfortune of being a girl after two boys, was put into Durga Bari.

The boys went to school on their bicycles, while Abdul, the rickshawala, was called in to take the younger girls to the school.

We bullied Abdul a whole lot; made him stop at the Mulberry bush, plucking those delightful sweet and sour shahtoot was a treat! Then we discovered that jungle jalebi (Manila tamarind) was another delight. If the jalebi turned out pink inside, it made our day, because then we could relish the sweet treat! Abdul would also help us pick the fruits and then share the spoils with us as evenly as we would let him. We would stand on the seats (where we were supposed to sit) and push and pull the thorny branches to get the fruit.

Abdul would be yelling, 'Bas, ab chalo!' but who was listening?

His final threat that would get us going would be 'Aaj toh Babuji ko bataunga. Bahut tang karte ho tum log!' (Today I will tell your father. You trouble me a whole lot!)

Abdul was a very patient man and he would never complain to Baba or Ma. He always managed to get us to school on time. On the way back he would carry our bags for us and hang them at the back of the rickshaw.

In the early days, our lunch used to be brought to the school by the servant Kanhaiya. A large reed mat would be spread under a tree. Out would come the plates, little bowls, spoons and glasses and the servant would dole out the food. It would be like a meal at home: the bhaja, the curry, the dal, salad and a fruit of the season.

I remember, that I once threw up after eating the apple; I could not stomach an apple for many years after that!

When I conceived my son and saw some apples in a shop, the aroma assailed my nostrils and I had this mad urge to bite into an apple. Fortunately, my dear mother-in-law had told my husband that he should provide me with whatever I asked for, else the infant would be forever hungry!

So, he got me an apple!

That of course broke the jinx!

***

Gaurav and Probir excelled in sports, like big brother Indrajeet and their father, Nobin. Of course, no one mentioned the similarities. Although Probir looked more like his father, yet Gaurav had the mental tenacity to excel in any sports he chose. And he chose tennis, like Indrajeet, and he did well. While he was being coached at the Alexander Club for tennis, he carried on playing hockey and football at school.

The Junior National Tennis Championship was scheduled for December when it was time for the final exams. Gaurav was given special permission to write his exam one week later. Since he was good at his studies, neither the school nor the parents were worried.

He came back with a shining Cup – the Junior National Championship Trophy in Tennis was his winning and Nobin's pride! For many years the cup had a pride of place in the spacious sitting room.

Probir was a good player of the game, yet he never could be as good as his elder brother, not in studies and not in games.

As they grew older, the sibling rivalry and envy stayed especially with Probir – the 'second child' syndrome really played out over the years!

The Annual Day or the Concert

The Annual Day was one of the school events that every kid looked forward to. Those who were to get on the stage were at once excited and nervous. Those who were to be the audience generally got free time under the supervision of a senior student.

Mrs Laing, my class teacher in Class IV, was also our music teacher. She would start practices for the school song a couple of months in advance. She was an Anglo-Indian who taught us the finer points of the school song: 'The school of St Mary's, our hope and our pride' we sang it so many times, it still reverberates in my head after nearly 50 years.

There were plays performed by the children of all the classes. Of course, the teachers were responsible for the selection, and the production of the plays. Since the parents were invited on this day, it was considered a very important function.

There would be two final rehearsals before the actual show. One would be for the final approval of the costumes and the whole show as such, to be judged by the Principal, then Brother Dooley. The second would be for the rest of the school. They had to walk down (in a single line!) up to Wheelers Club where they would sit on the floor. The chairs came in only for the final day! The parents came in on the Annual Day all dressed up in their Sunday best to watch their wards perform. This show would be held in the evening.

The other major event in the School Calendar would be the Sports Day, where every child had to participate. This was a daytime event, where again the parents were invited. The highlight for the parents would be watching the kids march to the Army band playing *Colonel Bogey's March*, and the prize distribution thereafter. The parents were then asked to stay back for tea.

Other than these two events, parents were never encouraged to come to the school, very unlike the monthly PTA meetings in schools today!

10

The Meerut Conspiracy Case and The...Murder Case

The Meerut Conspiracy Case was a controversial court case initiated in British India in March 1929 and decided in 1933. Several trade unionists, including three Englishmen, were arrested for organizing an Indian railway strike.

The British Government was clearly convinced that this was due to the infiltration of communist and socialist ideas propagated by the Communist Party of India (CPI). Remember the Communists were just coming into their own after the bloody revolution in Russia and were spreading their hold in India. The then government perceived, that it was the aim of the Communists to paralyze and overthrow existing Governments in every country (including India), by means of a general strike and armed uprising. The government's immediate response was to foist a conspiracy case – The Meerut Conspiracy Case.

In more ways than one, The Meerut Conspiracy case trial helped the Communist Party of India to consolidate its position among workers.

It also brought reflected glory to the Bar Council and the eminent legal fraternity of Meerut, where every young legal luminary worked that much harder to ensure that the city could retain the glow of being a good place to bring in a contentious issue and win.

Nobin began making waves in the legal world of the state. His expertise was spoken about in various circles. Clients came to him from faraway places and very often he would be travelling to Allahabad to argue in the District Courts, especially after having won in the Sessions' Courts of Meerut.

Nobin never discussed any of his cases at home at the dining table when the family sat down to dinner.

Then one of the kids asked one evening:

"Baba what has happened at the temple, near the old house? We cross it every day on our way to the school."

Nobin evaded the issue, "A new temple is coming up there. It is a Jain temple. Now who will tell me about the religion of the Jains?"

But I was like a dog rooting for an answer. Abdul had told us that there had been a murder there and Baba was their lawyer. He knew because another rickshawala was involved, someone who was an acquaintance of Abdul. That guy had run away from the servant's quarters of the old house near the temple.

That evening, I sat with Baba and asked him the question again; and also told him what Abdul had told us. I could make out that Baba was a little angry with Abdul for telling us these tales, but then the fact that I had come back to ask him, despite his efforts to shake us off, did carry weight with him. He liked to encourage my reading and the quest for learning more.

Baba would order the Reader's Digest condensed books for me, every couple of months. Many a times, he would ask me to read aloud from the newspaper for his friends or clients. I used to feel very chuffed!

Baba then explained, 'The Shah family that lives there are Gujarati Jains and follow a very strict regimen of fasting and praying. Jainism is an ancient religion, a contemporary of Buddhism, which has all but disappeared from India. Jainism has survived because the richest people in India, the Marwaris are all followers of this religion. Through their beliefs and their zeal for prayers, exquisitely built Jain temples are flourishing; a brilliant example is the Ranakpur temple near Udaipur.

'Jain temples are very rare; unlike Hindu temples that crop up everywhere, with our millions of gods. I guess Hindus have the freedom to build temples to whichever deity they favor.

'Now old Mrs Shah was deeply religious; and all her life she had had this recurring vision that she should build a temple for Bhagwan Mahavira. Her husband supported her idea and was ready to provide the money required for the same.

'The construction of the temple started in all earnest. Before it could be completed Mr Shah passed away. The money was flowing out in great chunks. The final 'shikhar' had to be done in gold or maybe plated in gold – that was to be the finale.

'There had been rumblings in the household because the daughter in law, Kamala, had been objecting to the overspending on the 'dream' project. She had been fighting with her husband, Nitin, trying to convince him that he should stop his parents from spending all the family's inherited fortune. She felt that it was a wasteful expenditure – she needed to keep some for the education of her boys.

'After the passing of her father-in-law, Kamala felt that her mother-in-law would give up chasing her dream. But the old lady was made of sterner stuff. Mrs Shah put herself into the project with even greater fervor.

'Now, Kamala had worked herself up to a frenzy, because her husband had paid no heed to her pleas. She then decided that she would have to take a major decision herself. Nitin was going to be out of town for a week.'

Just then, Baba got a call from Nitin Shah, asking for an appointment to see him.

Kamala, with the help of the rickshawala, Hassan, who lived in their servants' quarters, had actually killed the old lady. Kamala had held her mouth while Hassan had stabbed her. Hassan, the poor man, had panicked and run away after the deed was done.

Nitin was called by Kamala and was told that Hassan had killed her mother-in-law.

One week later, Hassan returned; dirty, bedraggled and hungry.

At the police station he had confessed to the murder but had said that Kamalaben had been instrumental in instigating the whole thing. And then he said the most incriminating thing – That she had held the old lady's mouth while he had actually stabbed her.

After a break of six months, I had the opportunity to sit with Baba once again. The case was going on. Nitin had been pleading with Baba that he should work his magic and ensure that Kamala should not be behind bars. Family izzat and all!

Sometime later I learnt from Baba's munshi that Kamala had been acquitted because the only evidence against her was that of a co-accused. Hassan was awarded life imprisonment.

After we heard this judgement, whenever we passed the house, we hoped to catch a glimpse of the lady; we never really did!

There is a kind of grisly curiosity about catching an actual glimpse of someone who has killed another!

11

The Relatives Arrive

Like in all large families, when one member establishes himself, the rest of the no good worthies follow to bask in the reflected glory.

Thus it was, that Nobin's elder brother Jyotindra followed him to Meerut, lock, stock, wife, with two boys and two daughters of marriageable ages. Fortunately, the two boys had had a semblance of education. So Nobin had them enrolled in the same Nanakchand High School, so they could get an Inter (Pass) Certificate. Nobin's contacts managed to get these two boys started in jobs so that they brought home some money for the sustenance of the family. Nobin was relieved as he was finding it difficult to stretch his resources – he had to look after his growing family as well as his brother's family.

On the other hand, another brother's widow, Satyavati, came to stay. She was a huge person and very finicky. She would wash all the taps with mud; purifying them because the sweeper 'may' have touched them! She had to do her own cooking separately in Kadambini's kitchen, in one little corner which she 'purified' by sprinkling water all over! That was also the time when none of the kids were allowed to enter the kitchen.

Another periodic visitor was Nobin's widowed sister, Charulata, who had been married when she was 10 to a man who was 15 years older than her, in keeping with the custom of those times. It was most unfortunate, that within a year of getting married, Charulata's husband died due to a sudden fever. She had been at her father's place in Gwalior ever since, living the life of a cursed widow. After her father's passing, the old house was sold and the 70 odd members of the family dispersed all over the country. The widows went to live with successful members of the family. Thus, Charulata and Satyavati came to Meerut.

Satyavati's educational qualifications extended to an Intermediate Pass in Hindi. This allowed her to teach in the primary school in Modinagar, once again courtesy Nobin's clients. She would then come home on weekends only, or whenever the school broke up for any kind of a vacation.

Charulata had no such qualification – so she stayed at home, helping Kadambini look after the girls. She would take great pleasure in oiling their hair and making tight plaits for them. She was the one who discovered that one of the girls had lice in her hair.

Kadambini was horrified!

The next day the family barber was called and he brought his kit to shave off the heads of all the four girls who were going to the convent. The older girls were saved because Charulata, the Pishima (father's sister), went through their hair with a fine-tooth comb and declared them free of the vermin!

The next morning the girls did not want to go to school, afraid they would be teased by the other kids. Kadambini found scarves for all four of them so they would not feel uncomfortable. On the quiet, she called up the school and told the headmaster that her daughters would be coming in to the school with their heads shaved because of the lice.

Maybe the other parents should get their children's heads checked.

The headmaster announced at the school assembly that some children were carrying lice in their hair, so they needed to get their hair cleaned out, else he would call for a barber and have him shave their heads.

***

The wedding season starts:

Jyotindra's two girls were older than Nobin's elder three girls, so an earnest hunt for grooms now began. Fortunately, eligible grooms were found for Jethababu's daughters and their marriages were solemnized in Nobin's own home.

Then it was the turn of Nobin's eldest girl, Meera, to tie the knot.

Meera, Archana, Indira and Kobita went to their school in the open horse carriage they had at home. The girls were young and pretty and many a youngster tried catching their eye. Meera recalled how one chap would ride his bicycle very close to the carriage; he would not say anything but just ride along; every morning, every school day! Quite different from today's street side Romeos who cannot stop spewing vulgarities!

Kadambini was very clear that she was not going to marry off her daughters to any old Ram Raghav or Rohit!! The groom had to be educated, had to have a government job (preferably IAS/IPS/IFS), and had to have a decent family background.

From, Hyderabad in South India came the Chatterjee family with a proposal for their second son, Amit who had all the specifications laid down by Kadamabini. He was a government employee and was well educated, although not an IAS/IPS/IFS!

Banerji sahib ki beti ki shadi hai! Was the excitement in the small mofussil town that Meerut was in 1956, Anyone who was anyone was present, including the rich industrialists from around the city.

I was all of 5years old and I had wet my new dress; yes, I had a problem of bed wetting till I was nearly 10 years old.

I recall that and I recall everyone going gaga over the gifts Didi had got. I had my first glimpse of a 'nylon sari' manufactured at Modinagar by Baba's industrial clients. The elders were raving over the colors and the finesse and how thin the fabric was! Even Ma was seeing something like this for the first time. Then there were many tea sets, loads of silver, some more rich Banaras saris.

The gifts Kadambini had readied for her first daughter were packed into trunks which were to travel with the newlyweds.

All the other gifts were packed into crates and dispatched to Warangal, along with the furniture gifted by the parents of the bride. The Chatterjee family was based there. What happened to all those gifts is enough to write a book about at a later stage!!

***

A little footnote here. That same year, in October 1956, the youngest (and prettiest!) of the Banerji girls was born.

One year later, around the same time, Meera's first son arrived.

For those who missed it, while Kadambini was carrying out the rituals for her first daughter's wedding, she was expecting her last child!

The difference between Kadambini's first grandson and her own youngest child was actually just a year! Calculations show that Kadambini had a full 24 years of child bearing! Her first born in 1932 and the last born in 1956.

***

Nobin's second daughter was married to an IAS officer from Gwalior, in 1959.The third daughter got an option to go to the UK on a work visa, so her wedding was delayed.

The next wedding was held in the summer of 1965. Kobita was married into an old zamindar family of Kolkata. She was all of 20 years old and her husband was a decade older than her. Kadambini had to move to Kolkata to her sister's place to find a suitable match for her...and find she did. It was a grand wedding indeed.

12

The Girls Grow – The Wolf Appears

The same year the wolf came into the lives of the younger girls.

It was not that he looked like a wolf or had violent tendencies. He was not a stranger; else he would not have got access to the inner sanctorum where the girls were. Yes – he was a relative; a young engineering student who was supposed to be a good football player too.

He was also a great spinner of yarns! He told tales which the naïve young girls swallowed. In their eyes he grew into a hero.

In Meerut the girls had led very sheltered lives; and after school hours had no interaction with the opposite sex. The brothers had already left for higher studies in Delhi; they only came home for the holidays. So, essentially, there was no other male in the house, other than Nobin.

Given this background to the girls' naïveté, the wolf had a field day.

He had started with one of the older girls.

One of the impressionable teen sisters had caught them at it and was dumb with shock. She could not talk about it to the other sisters – it just was not done…nor could you discuss such matters with Ma!

The girls had a very formal and proper relationship with their mother.

The girls read a lot of fiction, having graduated from the wholesome Reader's Digests to Harold Robbins' *79 Park Avenue* via Pearl S Buck's *The Good Earth*; their exposure to sex was mainly through books. Besides there was only 'moral science'; no sexual awareness lessons at school. Those came much later in the early 1960s when the Patrician Brothers had decided that they were not going to take any more girls after Class V. Once the senior girls passed out, the school would be for boys only.

Till then, the girls had to be given some tips on social etiquette and lessons on personal hygiene. So, the older teachers were told to put together the girls of Class VII upwards (basically those who had started their menstruation). It was quite obvious that the parents were not telling the girls anything about the changes that were happening in their bodies and what they meant! They had to be told why 'periods' happened and how to deal with the sanitary pads, as most were using homemade pads in those days.

It was the month of May and it was blistering hot outside! We were all sleeping on the floor in Ma's room, in Meerut where the big cooler was running. This was the coolest room in the house and all of us took our afternoon siesta here – Ma on her canopied bed, and all of us 'chillar' party on the floor, giggling and fighting till one word from Ma and would silence all. Ma would call me or Munnu as we two were considered the loudest and the noisiest!

I woke up with a start as I felt wet in my bloomers. I had a problem of bedwetting but that was at night! It had not happened during the day! What was wrong? I got up with a start and went to the en-suite bathroom.

I came out and called Mejdi. Ma also got up. They had a whispering session between themselves.

Ma: I was thinking that she would start any day. Teach her how to make the pad. Take out the white sari from the cupboard and show her.

Mejdi did just that – showed me how to wear the homemade pad. I had to get a string around my middle and on to the string would sit the pad; and then the bloomer was to be worn.

Nobody told me that this painful 'thing' would last a maximum of six days! Nobody said that I could get back to climbing trees.

I would be waddling around with that uncomfortable pad and feeling truly sorry for myself. I thought I was dying. Remember, readymade panties and sanitary pads were still a decade away! Besides, even when they did come into the market, they were quite expensive! Ma's old Bengal handloom saris had to do for us for many more years to come!

The only saving grace was that I could take a break from school! And that perplexed my brother; Gaurav never said anything, Probir did.

"Why are you not going to school? Nothing wrong with you! Just sitting around and eating all day!"

Ma heard that and came to my rescue. "Or shorir bhalo nayee! (she is not well)"

This particular phrase was the euphemism for "She has her periods! So, don't trouble her!"

Then one day, when Munnu also started her periods, Mejdi sat us down with the encyclopedia to explain with a handy diagram, what exactly was happening inside our bodies. She pointed out the uterus and told us that that was where babies were made. She added that when girls started their periods, it was nature's way of telling us that we were ready to have babies.

She did not mention how the babies got there so the whole process of making babies was left out, although to her credit, she did tell us that boys had to be kept at bay; they were part of the baby making process!

Nothing was said about the 'weird' sensations that dazed you if your vest touched your nipples. And then the breasts just grew and grew. What to do? How do you stop them? What do you do about them?

One fine day, Mejdi got me a bra designed to keep the jiggling and jumping breasts in place; also designed to help you run and play. Suddenly I was walking taller and straighter! Felt good!

In school there was one girl, Lakshmi, who was so obviously not wearing a bra; even the boys noticed. Mejdi who was our Sanskrit teacher told one of the senior teachers who called in Lakshmi's mother and explained the delicate situation.

One week later Lakshmi came into class wearing a bra under her chemise. Now the boys could relax and get on with their own issues instead of thinking about Lakshmi's breasts and the jiggling thereof; and what happened to their own nether regions and why did the trousers suddenly feel tight across the crotch!

The poor innocents knew there was some connection there, but what was it? No one ever told them! I guess they found out in their own sweet time!

There were no special classes for the boys to help them understand the changes in their bodies and accept their own adolescence.

***

"Bhiku is looking for you and he has a mean looking *khukhri* in his hand. You better run, Khoka, if you want to save yourself."

"Get up you idiot!"

Suddenly a blast of cold air hit Khoka's limbs as he felt his blanket being yanked off.

"Uthbi na morbi?" (Are you getting up or you want to die?)

Someone was shaking him awake and his head was hurting really badly. Khoka's eyes refused to open. Through that haze his subconscious recognized the panic in the rising crescendo of Bhanuda's voice.

He tried curling up, when suddenly, he felt a splash of cold water on his face!

"What…what…? *Ki holo Bhanuda*?" he sputtered, now wide awake.

"Bhiku is looking for you and he has a mean looking *khukhri* in his hand. You better run Khoka if you want to save yourself!"

"But what happened? Why is he looking for me?"

By now Khoka's head had cleared somewhat and through the haze surfaced images from the night before.

"Ah Gora! You are so beautiful – love your smooth skin which smells of sweat and roses. It is such a heady mix. I want to bury myself in you."

She had allowed Khoka to enter that curly forest below and they had made very tender love all night.

Khoka sat on the bed with an idiotic smile on his face, till another mug of cold water hit him.

Bhanuda came up close and snarled, "Get up and get out, Fucker! Enough of daydreaming!"

Khoka could smell the fear on his rancid breath.

Khoka pulled out his battered bag, dumped a few clothes in it and was ready to leave. But go where?

Why not *mashi's* house in Meerut? He surmised it was far enough and safe enough.

While he packed, Khoka decided to go to Asansol first; touch base with Ma and Baba, pack some decent clothes and then board the Rajdhani for Delhi.

Khoka's father, was surprised to see him. They had not expected to see him for the next couple of months; at least until the final exams were done.

Khoka told them that the Naxals were after his blood!

"We had a football match a few days ago with a local college. We were a better team and we were sure to win. But the local goons were cheering for the local team. Then they started turning violent; pushing, shoving and kicking, especially in the vulnerable body parts. There was this solidly built Muslim boy – Aslam – who was being cheered by the locals. This was adding to his rising arrogance.

"Some of my team mates had to be carried off the field. Then my team had a confab and we decided that we could not just stand by and watch.

"We decided to tackle Aslam in his own coin.

"I was dribbling and moving really fast. I lifted the ball out to pass it to Deepak, when, like a whirlwind, Aslam came charging at me; I had an inkling that he would try that. Unluckily for him, he caught the full force of my football boot on his face and went down in a heap.

"It was his turn to be carried off the field! Anyway, we won the match and we celebrated.

"I was woken up very rudely this morning and told that Bhiku, one of the local *dadas* was looking for me. I guess he wanted to get even with me for battering up Aslam. Later I heard Bhiku…never mind…so I felt that I would just come home for a few days!"

Baba was on the phone; Khoka could hear him shouting at someone.

"What is this nonsense? Who is this character who wants to kill my son? Can the College not protect him…? If my son does not clear his final exam, I shall hold the college responsible!"

Right! It was time to move before Baba got to the truth.

Ma walked in. "Listen Khoka, your *mejo mashi's* daughter is getting married in your *choto mashi's* house in South Kolkata. The wedding is in a week's time. Why don't you join them there instead of going to Meerut?"

Khoka felt that to be a wonderful idea; Kolkata still had some of his old friends…and then *mejo mashi* had all those nubile young daughters.

"Okay Ma; I will leave for Kolkata tomorrow. I will be back when I can…"

With that vague injunction, he left. Since it was only a short haul, Khoka took a bus and was in Kolkata by the evening.

***

8 Shambhunath Pandit Street was one of the old elegant homes of Bhawanipore, South Calcutta with three floors of stylized Anglo Oriental architecture with shining teak banisters and sparkling marble tiled floors. The walls had

black and white framed portraits of the ancestors; the dining hall had a massive dining table to seat at least 30 people.

Choto mashi was the very frail and delicate mistress of the manor; while *mesho moshai* (*mashi's* husband) was the quintessential *Bangali sahib* who wore Savile Row suits in England and a starched white *dhuti Panjabi* while in Kolkata – a very polished gentleman, very generous and large-hearted.

Their only child, Anita, was a sickly juvenile diabetic daughter, more like a frail ghost about the house. Thus, *mesho* was happy to have Kadambini's boisterous young family all over the place.

The mother and daughter lived on the second floor while *mesho* lived on the ground floor, just off the grand living room. The middle floor was where the elaborate dining table was placed. It was quite sad to see Anita with thick spectacles on her nose, going through some boiled food at one end of the table. She almost disappeared in that grand hall!

Just behind the main building was another building of three floors – this was where the huge kitchen and the living quarters for all the staff were located. The kitchen was on the middle level, connected to the dining hall by an open passageway; this made it easy for the servants to bring in the dishes to the table, especially if there were guests at any meal.

***

The wedding was an elaborate affair spread over four days. The guests were from a cross section of Calcutta's elite society.

All the rituals were done with a lot of ***hoi-hoi*** and always followed by great food.

"Gaye Holud" (the haldi ceremony) marked the beginning of the festivities. In order to make the bride and groom's skin

glow, they are made to sit on a *piri* (a flat wooden seat) placed on the floor and are rubbed with a turmeric paste by the married women of their respective families. Part of the turmeric paste used on the groom is sent to the bride's family along with the *piri.* The application of turmeric takes place after some mantras are recited.

The bride is made to wear *Shankha Paula,* which are special bangles made of shell and coral. They signify the status of a married Bengali woman.

Instead of *mehndi,* so common in North Indian weddings, Bengali brides apply a red pigment called *aalta* on their hands and the soles of their feet, as a symbol of Goddess Lakshmi who will bless her husband's home with wealth and prosperity.

Many non-Bengalis are very amused by the Bengali custom of ululating, called *hulhuli* in the local parlance! While most believe it is done to ward off evil spirits, it is also done as a signal for the beginning/end of important occasions and events. *Hulhuli* is usually accompanied by the blowing of the conch shell *(shankh)*.

Unlike most Hindu weddings, the wedding night in a Bengali wedding is not for consummation. That is when the younger members of the family keep the newly wedded couple awake with a lot of song and dance. It is called *baashor jagai* and everyone, including the bride, is encouraged to perform. These days a lot of practice goes into the 'show'!!

The day after the wedding is the *bashibiye*, where the couple are still at the bride's place and the groom puts some more sindoor in the bride's hair. After sunset, the couple are not supposed to see each other as the evening is considered *'kaal ratri' (the night of death)* – based on an ancient legend.

Now it is time for the bride to leave for her new home and to be welcomed by the parents-in-law, in a ceremony called *Bou Boron.* The mother-in-law greets the new bride with an *arati* and then the bride puts her feet into a plate filled with dye and milk. Then she walks with stained feet on a white sheet of cloth and enters her new abode.

The *Boubhat* brings the celebrations to an end. It is an event organized by the groom's family, nowadays called a "reception" to introduce the new bride to the entire family.

***

So, there were the guests of the groom's family, the Chatterjees, who were an old family of Calcutta; then there were the Banerjis of Shambhunath Pandit street, again another old family of Calcutta; the bride's family, the Banerjis from Meerut who would have been enough by themselves for any wedding.

So, all the *mashis,* (mother's sister) *meshos,* (*mashi's* husband) *kakus* (father's brothers) and *kakimas* (father's brothers' wives), and *Khokas,* (boys), *Khukis* (girls) were present *enmasse!*

Then there were the kids – the Meerut Banerji daughters and grandkids had been a restive noisy brat pack, with the little ones sliding down the shiny teak banisters of the house. Banerji of Kolkata would sit on one of the grand easy chairs in the carpeted sitting room and with a benign smile, look on.

In a side whisper, he told Banerji of Meerut, "I always wanted this big house to resonate with the laughter of kids. Nobin Da, you are so lucky, you have so many daughters who in turn will give you so many grandkids to fill your old age."

Nobin looked on as one of his daughters managed the noisy kids and yelled at them for being so difficult.

"Yes, I'm proud of my daughters. They are good with their studies and their games. They are all playing badminton now, you know. And doing well… Chatterjee *moshai* wants Kobita to play for West Bengal at the Nationals. Who knows…? She might do us all proud."

Nobin had always been proud of his children's achievement in games and sports. That his daughters should represent the states was a matter of great pride for him. As it is daughter number 5, Beni was getting ready to represent her state, Rajasthan, where she was playing for Jaipur University.

The two sisters did meet up in the Nationals of the year '67-'68. No one could have been more excited than their father, sitting in Meerut.

***

During the day, the wolf was present at all the ceremonies, helping and lending a hand where he could. While by night, he was into his predatory prowling!

Tutu, one of the school going girls, woke in the middle of the night to go to the loo. She had to pass through one of the rooms where the elder sisters and other cousins were sleeping.

She saw him working on one of the elder cousins – a bare bottom moving rhythmically up and down, while two slim legs were lying out straight. Although she had no carnal knowledge, yet she had read enough to know what was happening.

She was silent and tried to edge out of the room as silently as she had come. Her head was swirling – she knew this was what Harold Robbins spoke about in his books.

But what was the reason for the wet feeling between her own legs?

What was it that was making her heart beat so rapidly?

Why was she feeling as if she had walked into something dirty?

She held her own face and felt the warm flush?

What had she done?

***

Five years later

The wolf is in Meerut. He is drinking regularly now and has no job. He is spinning some more yarns. The latest story is that he is supposed to be chased by the Naxals who do not like his bravado. Mr Banerji gets him a job in Modinagar, where he has to make use of his engineering degree to earn his salary.

Yet every weekend he is back in the Meerut house, scaling the walls and coming down the staircase.

He goes and knocks on the last door that opens out on the verandah.

"Hey Tutu, open the door…*aami* (it is I!)"

From inside comes a hushed voice, "What are you doing here at this hour?"

"Open the door, I will explain!"

"No! I cannot!"

"Why?"

"*Pishima* is sleeping in the next room and she will wake up."

He heard a loud voice, "Kay? Who is there?"

Pishima was up.

"No one, *Pishima*, I was just going to the loo."

Quietly, Tutu opened the door and went out.

He was standing there.

She evaded him and went to the toilets attached to the verandah. He followed. She told him to go up the stairs and stay there, she would come. He smelt weird – a sickly sour smell! Was that alcohol? It must be! He also appeared unsteady on his feet.

She walked up to the terrace.

"You have no business coming into the house at this hour…in any case, how did you do it?"

He came halfway down the staircase and showed her – the pumphouse had a shallow roof, barely six feet off the ground. Any athlete could scale up to the roof. From there, one could land on the middle of the staircase, which was barely a hop and skip away. So, you could go either up or down.

"So, I came down to you."

He came closer, rubbing her arms, speaking softly and slowly.

"I knew you would not turn me away!"

She was spellbound! Even in the dark, his eyes shone with sincerity. He held her close while she rested her head on his shoulder. She shut her eyes.

All the romantic lines from all the books she had read came flooding in. No one had spoken to her like this. Her heart was beating rapidly and her anger and annoyance had melted away. She wanted him to hold her. She wanted to stay like this forever…

The books said the bells would start ringing! She would find herself in a beautiful meadow with mountains in the distance and a pretty little stream gurgling down the hillside. In a Hindi movie, a song would have started by now with the hero and heroine dancing around the trees!

She kept her eyes shut for the next two minutes, then she opened them wide and started laughing!

"Ki holo? Why are you laughing?"

"Can you hear some bells ringing somewhere?"

"No..."

"Maybe you were singing a song?"

"No..."

"Then the books are all wrong," and she laughed a nervous laugh.

He tried drawing her close so he could hold her against him, but she wriggled out as she was uncomfortable with her own rising emotions.

Besides, there was always the thought that someone would spot her! She ran off down the stairs and entered the bedroom silently.

He then wandered off to his bed in the solitary room on the terrace.

Another time...another day...

***

A pleasant Sunday morning in October...Nobin and Kadambini were heading to Delhi for a wedding. The younger two daughters were more than happy driving down to Delhi.

Tutu had a pile of exam papers to correct – remember…she was a teacher at her Alma Mater, St Mary's Academy.

The wolf was still asleep in the attic room.

***

He had been watching the departure of the family from the terrace. He had counted the heads and had realised that one was missing.

He went back to his room and lit up a cigarette; some planning needed to be done. After all seduction had never been an easy game!

He sauntered down the staircase in his lungi. He was there in the verandah and called, *"Ayee, Paresh, cha dibina?" (Paresh no tea for me?)*

No one came out or responded.

"Tutu, where are you? Is no one at home?"

She poked her head out of her room.

"There is no one at home…you want tea, you know where the kitchen is. Go and get it yourself."

He put on his lost boy look. "But I don't know where the tea is…" his voice trailed off.

"Then go look for it…!" she yelled and went back to her work.

She heard some pottering around in the kitchen. A loud 'clang' told her the pots were falling out of the dish rack.

The fridge was opened. Another yell, "Where is the milk?"

"In a stainless-steel pot on the top shelf."

"I can't see it."

She came storming out of the room, "You guys cannot see anything!"

She moved a few things around and gave him the vessel with the milk.

Then she took it back, poured some milk into a tumbler and gave it to him. Very coolly she then put it back into the fridge.

"Now make your tea and give me a cup also!"

"Hey before you go, tell me where is the tea and the sugar?"

"Oh God!" she groaned. "I may as well make the tea…" she grumbled.

Silently, she made the tea and handed him a cup. She carried her own cup to her room and shut the door.

Fifteen minutes later –

Knock knock!

"Please open the door Tutu."

"What do you want? Let me do my work!"

"I need some money…please give me some money," he whined.

She took out a 100 rupee note from her purse and opened the door.

"Here take this and don't trouble me anymore…by the way…what do you want it for? If you are looking for something to eat there is enough of bread and butter and eggs."

"No. I want to get some beer…and I want you to share it with me."

He looked at her with his little lost boy look, the one that would melt the heart of a tartar! And a tartar Tutu was not.

She was very sensitive and a soft touch; she did not know how to say 'no' to anything, leave alone to this wily cousin who knew how to manipulate the heart strings of a young virgin!

She had lost count of the number of times he had extracted 100 rupees from her – maybe she should keep a track of things; but since she had never told anyone else about this habit of the cousin, she would have to keep quiet or face humiliation. Ma would be very angry, as she was dead against any drinking in the house.

"What are you thinking, beautiful?"

"Stop saying that…I'm not beautiful!"

"Who says you're not? You have beautiful doe eyes and your skin is so soft and clear…"

While saying this he had edged into the room and had come close to her…really close…

"Stop flattering me," she said in a small voice, while he held her close and kissed her softly on the forehead.

She could feel her heart pounding…he kissed her on her eyes.

"Such beautiful soulful eyes you have…"

She was melting and felt her entire body crumbling, succumbing, to this sensuous feeling.

He was kissing her on her lips now…she could smell the tangy Binaca toothpaste. He had moved down to her neck and she was letting him do it…his hand rested on her breast and then slowly moved downwards…

Very gently and delicately he took off her clothes and lay her down on the bed. He took off his lungi and kept it aside.

She had never seen a naked man before...the size of his engorged penis worried her...was all of that going to enter her? No...how could it?

He extracted a small packet from his trouser pocket, took out a small white flat balloon and wore over his penis.

"What is that?"

"A condom... also called a French Letter..."

"What is it for?'

"So that you do not get pregnant."

He saw her watching him and his body. He said softly, "Don't worry I will not hurt you. If you feel any pain tell me and I will stop."

He was experienced and she was a raw virgin; he knew all the right buttons to press.

It was a first time for her and she was uncomfortable to say the least.

But the second and third time it became pleasurable.

His fingers grazed her nipples and she arched...his fingers slowly travelled down her stomach to her core and she felt a shiver of pleasure...his fingers went down to her wetness and she groaned...

They had all day to spend and he knew that he could have his way with her whenever he wanted.

He was prepared and seemed to have many little packets of condoms tucked away in some pocket or the other.

***

It became quite the routine.

During the week he would stay in his one room apartment in Modinagar. He never brought any money home – most of his salary was spent on liquor. On Friday evening he would be back to carry on his night-time rendezvous with Tutu.

She looked forward to it.

Saturday was the day for *mashi* to be driven to Kalibari. If Khoka had got over his weekend hangover, he would happily drive her over.

She would stop to buy vegetables and he would ask her for some money.

"*Mashi ek tu poisha daona…*" (give me some money) again, with that little lost boy look.

Now Kadambini had the brood of girls; her sons had already left for higher studies, and here was this surrogate son asking for some money.

"What do you want to buy?"

"I want to buy some kababs from the *sardarji*'s *dhaba* across the road."

She would have denied her daughters kababs from the *sardarji*'s *dhaba* and would have said that it was dirty because it was on the side of the road and they would be sick! But then how could she deny her sister's son? *Bechara…*

He got the money and got the kababs. At home, with tea, he convinced his *mashi* also to enjoy the kababs.

***

Almost every evening when Khoka was at home, he would drink on the quiet, after extracting some money from Tutu or his *mashi*.

Then to please Kadambini he would sing bhajans for her – old and new Bangla songs, Nazrul *geeti*, Rabindra sangeet, Ramprosadi (bhajans in praise of Kali). Nazrul *geeti* were patriotic songs written by a Muslim cleric from erstwhile East Bengal. Kadambini would then ask Tutu to join in, as she had a good singing voice and a master was coming to train the girls.

The song session pleased Kadambini no end –she loved music although she herself could not carry a note. Nobin could sing and would often join in the music evenings.

Soon it became quite the routine. The evening music sessions gave Kadambini a pleasant break from her routine. She looked forward to it. It gave the nephew one more reason to stay away from work and enjoy his hedonistic lifestyle. Why should he slog when all his basics were looked after? Was there any responsibility added to this sybarite? None whatsoever!

He made the most of it while he could.

13

The Tale of Three Nations

December 1971

It was all coming to a head.

August of 1947 saw the partition of India; the land was divided on the basis of religion. West Pakistan was culled from almost all of the Punjab; and East Pakistan was made up of most of erstwhile Bengal. Within the year Mohammad Ali Jinnah was dead.

On a whim and a firm belief that History would always remember him as the man who carved out a nation for Muslims, I would like to believe that he must have been turning in his grave when he saw his dream crumbling. The partition of India on the basis of religion was probably one of the greatest blunders of the 20th century.

All the Muslims in India did not want to go to Pakistan; and all the Hindus in Pakistan did not want to migrate to India. Nearly11 million people died in this chaos caused by the idea of one megalomaniac. Unfortunately, all the peaceniks never saw this coming: the scale of the death and the horror of 1947-48 could have been at par with the persecution of the Jews by Hitler during and before the Second World War.

Both were done in the name of religion.

Jinnah had wanted all of Bengal also to be a part of Pakistan, but then Shyama Prasad Mukherji stepped in and saved

Calcutta, which was then considered the richest city of the East. Thus, East Bengal consisting of many predominantly Muslim areas – like Sylhet (Assam), Chittagong, Noakhali and others became East Pakistan.

The Hindus chose to stay on there.

The statistics are mind numbing. Within three decades of Independence the percentage of minorities in both the parts of Pakistan had dwindled, while in India they thrived.

There were rumblings in East Pakistan, where there was a cry for some kind of democratic freedom from the shackles of the Pathan ruling class of West Pakistan. The Awami League had formed under Sheikh Mujibur Rehman and the rising crescendo of discontent forced elections in the East.

The **Bangladesh War of Independence**, or simply the **Liberation War** in Bangladesh, was a revolution sparked by the rise of the Bengali nationalist and self-determination movement. It resulted in the independence of the People's Republic of Bangladesh.

The war began after the Pakistani military junta based in West Pakistan launched Operation Searchlight against the people of East Pakistan on the night of 25 March 1971. It pursued the systematic elimination of nationalist Bengali civilians, students, intelligentsia, religious minorities and armed personnel. The junta annulled the results of the 1970 elections and arrested Prime minister designate Sheikh Mujibur Rahman. The war ended on 16 December 1971 after West Pakistan surrendered.

An estimated ten million Bengali refugees fled to neighbouring India, while thirty million were internally displaced.

The **Indo-Pakistani War of 1971** took the shape of a military confrontation between India and Pakistan that occurred during the Liberation War in East Pakistan from the 3rd December 1971 to the fall of Dacca (Dhaka) on 16 December 1971. The war began with preemptive aerial strikes on 11 Indian air stations, which led to the commencement of hostilities with Pakistan and Indian entry into the War Of Independence in East Pakistan on the side of Bengali nationalist forces. Lasting just 13 days, it is one of the shortest wars in history. (Wikipedia)

The earlier wars with Pakistan had not brought the Indian Air Force into the limelight. This one did. The heroics of Paramjit Singh Sekhon who was decorated with the Param Vir Chakra posthumously, became legendary. The fighter pilots of the IAF became great heroes in their blue G-suits and their faster-than-sound fighting machines. Till then, very little had been heard of them and their gallantry.

Within six months, the movie *Aradhana* hit the movie theatres, starring Rajesh Khanna (the then popular heart throb and superstar) and Sharmila Tagore.

Every young unattached woman fell in love with the dashing Rajesh Khanna who enacted both the roles of fighter pilot father and son. It was a typical Hindi movie with a lot of song and dance and picturesque landscapes of the Kashmir valley.

14

The Other Love Story

Tutu was in love with the image of love, projected by the movie and the circumstances of the war. The glamour of the 'flyboys' could not be ignored. She knew it was unreal, that all celluloid stories were far removed from reality. But then, romantic by nature, and sensitive to the environment, she found it hard to remain practical and sensible.

Even though she was having that quiet affair with her cousin she was getting quite tired of trying to hide it. Moreover, she was also getting tired of having to spend her meager teacher's salary on maintaining her 'lover'. She hated the word!

She wanted to now get out of the family home and have her own home and husband, perhaps children.

At this juncture in the story, it is important to recall that Kadambini Devi was very clear that all of her brood of kids were going to marry into proper Bengali Brahmin families – there was no question of marrying out of that narrow boundary of caste and language. Yet, marriage of her girls was the be all and end all of her existence. She thought of very little else.

There were regular saree vendors coming to the house every six months. They knew there was a captive market here. Then Manik Babu the small-time goldsmith and full-time wedding broker walked in every few months. There was always some trinket to be refashioned, some clasp to be put in place or a ring that had a stone missing.

Another regular visitor once again, was the astrologer cum pandit, who would look at auspicious details of various sorts and decide whether a certain proposal was worth following up or not. Then there were the various '*patros*' or the possible grooms. Sometimes, someone was coming from Bombay or Delhi to 'see the girl', sometimes Kadambini was going off to Calcutta to see a possible groom with one daughter or other in tow!

Imagine the humiliation the girl suffered if the almighty 'possible groom/*patro*' rejected the girl after meeting her and subjecting her to endless questions.

So, after seeing Beni suffer all these humiliations, Tutu had decided that she was not going to go through this for anyone. She did it once and she had the pleasure of turning down the proposal because the precious candidate was short fat and ugly! So, what if he was a Bengali Brahmin!? So, what if his lineage was of the very best!?

Kadambini smiled to herself because she was not partial to this particular *patro* herself! She agreed with Tutu's descriptions

***

When the school announced that an excursion to Srinagar was being planned during the summer break of 1972, Tutu was the first one to register for it. Although it was meant mainly for the kids the two senior teachers who were going along as managers did not deny her a place. After all they had been her teachers, not so many years ago! For them she was a little older than the other kids.

So, the first part of her dream romance had been put in place! Not that she thought of it like a part of a plan…but just thinking of the beautiful valley, the mountains, the rivers, the flowers and fruits and the idyllic Dal Lake made her love it already without ever having been there!

Tutu had called up Flight Lieutenant Tyagi, a family friend from the IAF, to check with him if he knew of a family where the lady could take them out shopping. The Kashmiris could spot a tourist a mile away and could cheat them. She did want to buy a few Kashmiri silk saris. He gave her a number for the AF exchange where she could ask for Flight Lieutenant JK Singh.

The train journey was very exciting as this was her first outing without the parents and the family. She felt one with all the kids – 13-15-year-olds who were all as excited as she was, to be going to the famous Srinagar valley. She did not feel much older than the kids as both Mrs Cyprian and Mr Yadav treated her also at par with them.

The last leg of the journey was by bus from Jammu to Srinagar. The kids were happy singing along with Tutu and Irene, the other unmarried teacher. They sang catchy Hindi movie songs with great enthusiasm! Fortunately, no one was sick or pukey over the circuitous mountain trails.

They reached Srinagar and were driven to their hotel Lakeview, in the Rajbagh area. It was a cute home which had recently been converted into a hotel. All the twenty kids and four teachers were accommodated.

***

The telephone rang at the crew room at the air base.

The old-fashioned telephone made a loud shrill sound. All the boys were sitting out in the sun enjoying the balmy weather. Tea and snacks had been served to them under the sprawling chinar tree.

NCE Muniram came to Squadron Leader Sadarangani and said, "Sahib exchange *aapse baat karna chahtey.*"

He went in and picked up the phone.

"Sir there is one lady on the line and she wants to speak to Flight Lieutenant JK Singh. When I told her there is no JK Singh here she said that maybe she had got the initials wrong. Is there any other Singh?"

Sadarangani took the call and found himself listening to a well-modulated gentle voice asking for JK because F/L SS Tyagi said he was here.

"I'm sorry Ma'am JK has left the Squadron some time ago. We do have one AJ Singh attached to us but he is in Ambala at present."

The voice was now beginning to sound deflated.

Sadarangani, ever the gentleman, said "Ma'am is there anything I can do to help?"

By now all the boys had trooped in and were milling around the Flight Commander. They had understood there was a woman at the other end of the line

"Is AJ Singh likely to get back soon?"

"He is expected back tomorrow. Maybe you could talk to him around this time tomorrow."

"Thank you. I will call again."

When the telephone rang the next day, the exchange connected directly to the crew room.
"May I speak with F/L AJ Singh please?"

"I'm sorry but he is not here. Who is calling please?"

Sadarangani had taken the call and knew it was the same young lady who had called earlier.

By now the younger lot of pilots were back hovering around Sada.

One grabbed the handset and spoke in his most mellifluous voice, "I know F/L Tyagi and F/L JK Singh personally. I am F/L Chetan Khanna; can I help you in any way?"

"Well…um…actually I am here with a school group and F/L Tyagi had said I could go with Mrs JK for some shopping of saris. I don't know if you can help – I'm sure you don't know anything about local silks, do you?"

"I can find out and take you to a reasonable shop."

"Oh, will you do that? That would be wonderful!"

"When do you want to go?"

"Today if possible? Because tomorrow morning we are leaving for Gulmarg."

"Fine, I shall be at your hotel by 4. I will bring along another friend and we shall be on two separate bikes."

"Great! My friend Irene is also keen to come. Oh, before I confirm I will have to take permission from the teacher in charge."

They rang off. Behind the scenes:

Chhotu exclaimed excitedly, "Hey Gur! I am good with Anglo girls so you take Ms. Banerji as your pillion and I will go with Irene."

"Hey! Did she say anything about these two being teachers or students?" asked Gur.

"If they are school kids, I'm sure there are teachers too; *unko pata lenge,*" said the irrepressible Chhotu, refusing to be quelled. "She did say something about a 'teacher in charge' and 'taking permission'! Let's go and check it out!" he added with a sly grin!

***

Their motorbikes roared into Lakeview. All the kids were out of their rooms and hanging over the balconies. Irene and I came down the wooden staircase in a grand flourish of chiffon saris and perfume. I sat down with Chhotu and Irene sat pillion to Rana.

All of Chhotu's grandiose plans had come to nought!

We drove around the Dal Lake; the boulevard with the lake on one side and elegant houses on the other was adorable. The backdrop of the Pir Panjal range was like a picture postcard. The boys took us to one sari shop on Residency Road, which was where tourists did all their shopping! And we believed we were getting bargains!

In the evening we planned to go to a local discotheque. Once again, these same two came to pick us up and took us to the Air Force Officers' Mess at Badamibagh so named because of the massive almond orchards in that area.

A beautiful wooden structure with parquet flooring in the lounge, it was a throwback to the romantic dances that were so much a part of the Royal Air Force. Of course, there was no dance going on, but just sitting there on the balcony overlooking the gardens while a waiter served these gallant young men, I think I was already a wee bit in love with the environment and the persona of these two dashing fighter pilots.

Remember my head was still swimming with Rajesh Khanna and 'Aradhana' and of course 'mere sapnon ki rani kab aayegi tu…' and then this guy was at least a Khanna if not Rajesh himself!!

The next day the group was leaving for Gulmarg and Pahalgam where we were to spend one night each. It was a dream holiday with nary a worry and only rosy romantic dreams.

Chhotu had asked me when we were getting back and that we could have dinner together before our departure the next day. It was something to look forward to.

Sure enough, we connected shortly after getting back and when Chhotu and Gur came in the evening, the kids came rushing to tell us, "Miss your 'vroom vroom' friends are here," this with graphic movements of hands and legs accompanied by matching sounds from the mouth!

Irene and I laughed and joined the fly boys in the portico where their booming bikes were bringing the house down…and how I loved it!

The evening passed in a haze. We went for a shikara ride where I sang a song. Then we had dinner and went dancing and finally walked for hours around the lake. I do not know what Gur and Irene spoke about but Chhotu and I talked endlessly about families, about my siblings, my school and whatever else we could share.

By the end of the evening, we had made promises which we intended to keep. The squadron was to get back to Ambala and Chhotu promised to visit Meerut.

Meanwhile I had applied for an air hostess' job with Air India. I was hoping I would make the grade because I was now bitten by the travel bug.

I first travelled when I was nearly fifteen, between New Delhi and Old Delhi, by the Rajdhani Express which Ma was supposed to catch for her annual visit to Kolkata.

Then the first ever long-distance train journey was when I finished with my School Leaving Certificate (Senior Cambridge) and Munnu and I were allowed to visit Kolkata. Everyone, that is my mashi and mesho, my didi and jamaibabu (didi's husband) and both my brothers, had been told that these two girls were coming and they needed to be looked after.

We stayed with my didi and had a great time. This was also the first time when we attended an adult New Year's Eve party in the high society of Kolkata.

I had never seen so many people in a three-bedroom flat! I guess the only people I had seen so milling around had been at weddings and many years later, at the discotheques so popular at the time. I recall I wanted to use the washroom and nearly tripped over bodies on the way. Even in the loo there were couples plastered on the walls. Then, when my brothers felt we had had enough they wanted to drop us home. One man in the lift wanted us to go with him and not go home as the night was still 'young' and we should have some 'fun'!

Fortunately, our brother saved us and dropped us to my didi's place a little after midnight!

Now, if I got into Air India, I could travel all over the world, and I would be free of Meerut and the insidious and discomforting liaison I had.

I did not become an Air Hostess though, because my parents refused to let me sign a bond for five years, a mandatory condition at that time.

15

Marry a Punjabi? Unthinkable!

Chhotu and I started writing letters, and he came to visit Meerut. He asked me to marry him. He had spoken to his mother and told her about me.

"*Bangalan hai*, mummy."

His mother was quiet for a while.

"So, what are you thinking Mum?"

"If you have liked her and chosen to marry her, she must be a good girl...but..."

Another long pause...

"But what Ma?"

"I'm worried! You have a temper and I don't know how she will cope with it."

"No Ma I have cooled down a whole lot...the fauj has sobered me down!"

Meanwhile in Meerut...

Ma would have nothing of it. no daughter of the Banerjis was going to marry a non-Bengali and that too, not a Brahmin. No one said anything about him being a Fighter Pilot in the IAF. To be honest no one knew anything about the Air Force!

Baba had worked with the Indian Army on a few Court Martials. He knew the Brigade Commander in Meerut and was proud of his acquaintance with him.

Chhotu came to visit my parents to do the right thing – ask their permission to marry me.

I was on pins and needles!

My father had played hockey and football in his younger days and could still pack a punch. I was half afraid my poor Chhotu might be at the receiving end of one such kick or fisticuff!

Our sitting room, called a 'drawing room' as in yesteryears, was a large square room with large windows near the entrance, neatly laid out sofas in a square with a long rectangular centre table. My father paced on one side of the centre table while Chhotu paced on the other – matching my father's steps. My father, being the lawyer, spoke best when he walked and he was trying his best to convince this young man that such a marriage was a difficult proposition.

Where was I?

Standing behind the curtains of the attached dining room, with one end of the curtain in my mouth, trying to stem my anxiety. I understood my father's anxiety – this was outrageous! How could he let his daughter marry a Punjabi?

No one had done this before! Yet secretly Baba liked the gumption of this young man with a big mustache; Baba and Ma had gone trudging around the country looking for suitable grooms for their daughters. And here was this smart personable young man, with a government job!

So what if he was not a Bengali? And so what if he was not a Brahmin? He would have to work on his wife's mindset. He was quite confident he could convince her, that is if she could not convince me to give up this stupid plan first.

I wrote a letter to Baba and left it under his pillow for him to read. He answered my letter with a letter of his own – describing his anxiety about marrying into a culturally different milieu. He was upset to read one of Chhotu's letters in which he had written that 'no son of a gun could stop us getting married'. He thought it was foul language. I knew it was not, so when I told this to Chhotu, he promptly wrote a most courteous letter to Baba apologizing and explaining that the term was not abusive, it meant 'a happy go lucky person'.

Meanwhile our letters between Ambala and Meerut carried on, as did my letters to my father. Once in two months or so, Chhotu would come down from Ambala and I would skip school for a couple of hours to sit behind a church so we could talk freely.

Then his sister, who had married a South Indian, came to visit. Now this South Indian brother-in-law, Muralidhar, was a very gregarious personality and a very smooth talker. He and Baba spoke at length and even though Baba made no commitment, he declared that Baba would be doing a great service to the nation by breaking down the barriers of caste and community.

The final parting shot was that since the young people had decided to get married, they may leave the home and do the right thing. So, would it not be better if the elders gave their blessings and allowed them to start their new lives on a positive note?

Baba said, "Yes, I know girls do that and many weddings have taken place like that. Let us see what happens."

***

Anyway, the wedding took place in true Bong style, although we did have a few very filmy kinds of sequences. My mother-in-law (bless her soul) wanted him to wear a suit and ride a mare in the wedding procession. I had asked him to wear a dhoti and kurta and he did wear the topor (the long elaborately carved headgear so typical to a Bong wedding!)

Murali bhai sorted the issue of the horse /mare by convincing our mutual mother-in-law that one could not find a mare at such a short notice since no one had told the girl's family that a horse would be required.

That would have been quite a sight – my Fighter Pilot riding a horse for his wedding dressed in a dhoti and a kurta, which would have hitched up to his knees and his hairy legs exposed to the whole world and their uncle!

The squadron boys ribbed him no end; and many an evening was spent recalling the horrors of the evening.

Of course, there were the lighter moments also. While the pujari chanted the prayers and our hands were clasped together, Murali bhai, kept intoning, 'haath mein haath daba lo" in the same manner as the pujari's sing song chant. I had a tough time curbing my giggles. The whole Khanna clan had come and were very amused at the goings on, especially when all the married women of my family started the 'ulu'.

The eldest member of the clan was Chhotu's maternal grandmother who was 80 plus and completely blind. She came and sat next to me and with her delicate and gnarled fingers traced my face and then hugged me.

Chhotu's younger brother, Akbar, a Major in the Indian Army came and quietly whispered to me, "Bhabhi find me a girl like you! Please!"

***

I went away to my new destination, to a new family who took me to their hearts in a wholehearted way.

***

Chhotu and his family had insisted they wanted nothing, but Tutu insisted that she wanted her saris and jewellery her mother had made for her. Her mother had also insisted on all the basics of a starter kitchen which was a great help to the young couple who had started their home life from scratch.

The young couple celebrated their first wedding anniversary with an infant son nearly two months old.

In the interim, Akbar's regiment moved to Meerut and he became a regular visitor in the Banerji household.

And the wolf went back to his old tricks. He had started working on Mithu, the sister two years younger than Tutu. In fact, at one time, he had worked on the two of them together…under the same blanket; and neither sister spoke about it to another or to each other.

Shame? Jealousy? Who knows?

Fortunately for Mithu, her wedding was fixed soon after Tutu's, to a Bong Brahmin and all. Kadambini went overboard selecting her jewellery, her saris and furniture for her new home.

***

After Mithu left with her new husband, the youngest sister, Lata, was left all alone. She still had to finish her post-graduation in English Literature from the local girls' college. Fortunately for her, the wolf was kept at bay by Akbar who became very close and protective about her. He had been a great help during Mithu's wedding.

Then one fine day, he declared to her parents that he wanted to marry their youngest daughter.

All hell broke loose!

How can he even think like that?

Rather how dare he think like that?

She was their precious child! The youngest and the prettiest, how dare he?

Tempers were roiling over and Kadambini was in no mood to listen to any logic or reasoning. She worked hard to find IAS officers (Bong Brahmins!) for Lata to take her mind off the smart young Major. Unfortunately, they all turned out to be dark, ugly, bespectacled and fat!

Benita who had been married the year before Tutu had also come for Mithu's wedding. She became an advocate for this wedding and tried reasoning with her mother.

She tried to clinch the argument by saying, "But you liked Chhotu and Akbar is his younger brother, they come from the same family. So, what have you got against him?"

"No Chhotu is a better person, always well-mannered and polite. Akbar is not."

This did not cut any ice with Benita. The three confabulated and figured out a way to get the young couple married anyhow – if not in Meerut, then Delhi would have to do.

Akbar's eldest sister and eldest brother were based in Delhi and they agreed to have a quiet ceremony. Beni would stand in for her parents.

No one in the family really believed that this chit of a girl would actually elope and marry.

But she did.

One year later, both Tutu and Lata were expecting. Tutu for the second time, Lata for the first. They met up in Secunderabad at their common sister-in-law's place.

The Indian Army and the IAF met and rocked – there were noisy celebrations in expectation of the arrival of the two babies and these two heavily pregnant sisters were more than happy to join in.

BOOK II

Introduction

Among eleven million people who were displaced before and after 1947, was the family of the Khannas from Lahore in Pakistan.

Hindus and Sikhs killed Muslims; and Muslims in turn, slaughtered the Hindus whenever they could and wherever they could. Carnage in the name of religion had never been worse; or perhaps it matched what Hitler did to the Jews in the years of the World War II. However, the latter case was one of planned genocide…a megalomaniac's 'vision' of a superior Aryan race; whereas, the killings of the Partition were a result of sheer mob frenzy driven by the insane urgings of bigots. Girls were raped and killed; trainloads of dead bodies drove into stations where fleeing families were waiting to go to the other side.

1

The Malhotras

Varanasi, Pathar ki Haveli – 1890

The Kapoor family had a flourishing business of hand-woven saris. These saris found a ready market with rich clans across the country. The three stalwart sons of the family had their work cut out – they ensured that their priceless hand woven zari saris reached discerning customers in the North, West and the Indo Gangetic plains, as far East as Calcutta, which was the hub of British India.

The country had recovered from the ravages of the Sepoy Mutiny and the party scene had picked up. Many an evening one could spot the bright lights of the Great Eastern Hotel, lighting up the Streets. Weekends were reserved for social gatherings where Indian merchants and British *burra sahibs* would be seen hobnobbing together.

The Indian women were usually seen wearing the rich Benaras silks with intricate workings of gold on the borders and little motifs all around.

The other great favourite was the chamois satin saris with *'gara'* work worn by the Parsi women. The Parsis were great traders who travelled regularly to China and Indonesia to source the silks and laces so popular with rich Indian women.

Although the Kapoor brothers were not in the same social league, they were happy to note that their saris were worn on many a fancy occasion.

Jatto Rani was getting married. She was the eldest of the four daughters of the well to do Kapoor family of Benaras and since she had already turned 12, it was high time she 'settled down'.

She was a petite, slim little girl who was shivering as the time drew near. She knew that there was a *dulha* (bridegroom) involved, and that her *kurmayi* (wedding) was happening. Beyond that Jatto Rani knew nothing. She had overheard some of the elders talking about Lahore and what a fabulous city she was going to live in.

The excitement of the new gold encrusted clothes and the jewellery had worn off; while the fear and anxiety had begun to trickle in. The fun and hilarity of the *sangeet* was also ebbing now.

The *jaimala* (the wedding garland)...the *pheras* (going around the fire)...and then...the *vidai* (time to say goodbye).

Jatto wept copious tears. Her anxiety overflowed and she clung to her mother and cried her heart out. Then her father intervened; and when she knelt down to touch his feet, he gathered her up in his arms and said, "*Betiyaan pair nahin chhootin, betiyaan ma baap ki izzat hoti hain.*" (daughters do not touch the parents' feet, they bring respect to the parents.)

Down the road, that injunction would carry – and would translate into love and affection for all the women in the family – daughters, daughters-in-law, mothers and wives.

Jatto and her newly minted husband Lajjya Ram Malhotra were sneaking shy looks at each other. They were actually seeing each other for the first time. Lajjya liked what he saw. Jatto had a creamy skin, a sharp classical nose and her hands were so tiny. In fact, she was altogether so tiny!

Meanwhile Jatto would have done some screening of her own and discovered that her husband was a 'big' man in more ways than one. He occupied nearly half the rear seat of the Plymouth they were being driven in – not that Jatto Rani knew where they were going, but she felt secure with this large man.

Lajjya Ram heard a tiny whisper of words from his new bride. She said, "Where are we going?"

He had to lean in to hear her and so he asked her to repeat what she had said. She cleared her throat and said in a stronger voice in Punjabi, "Where are we going?"

He smiled and held her hand through all the heavy jewellery and the veils. In a gentle voice he said, "We are driving down to Lucknow from where we will catch a train to Bhusawal. Have you ever been in a train?"

He felt, rather than saw, an imperceptible shake of the head. Then he felt the grip on his hand tightening and he understood her fear.

This child he had married, had hardly ever gone out alone in her hometown. She was now entering a whole new world so far removed from her own sheltered and protected life. He would have to be very patient and induct her into the family very slowly.

So, he began to tell her about their stops in Lucknow and Bhusawal – and their final destination Lahore. He told her all about Lahore, about their home in Ghas Mandi, how many rooms there were, and all the people who lived there. He told her about how Diwali and Holi were celebrated. He continued to describe his home and his beloved city, when he suddenly felt her head droop on his shoulder.

She had fallen asleep.

He put his arm around her in a protective gesture and shut his own eyes.

Lahore lived up to all of Lajjya Ram's descriptions and more. Sometimes Jatto missed Ganga '*maiyya*', and the temples and noise of the ancient city which was her hometown. Very soon she became a part of the rambunctious Malhotra family where music and dance, were of a piece with the main business of grain and the buying and selling of it. Large joint families celebrated every festival with great gusto.

Within the first two years of her marriage, Jatto Rani gave birth to her beautiful daughter who had all the classic beauty of the Punjabi ancestors. She was named Padmavati and she grew into a very happy child nurtured by all the older women of the family.

Two years later, Jatto Rani gave birth to another daughter who was named Nandrani.

The son and heir, Ram Lubhaya, was born after a gap of nearly ten years.

2

The Khanna Brothers of Lahore

In another upper crust area of Lahore city, very close to the Grand Palace, was the massive family home of the Khannas; where the four boys were being groomed in the true tradition of royalty. Their father was a high ranking official in the court of Maharaja Ranjit Singh.

The boys were all very handsome with all the fine features of their ancestors. It was understood that they would be educated abroad, probably in England, and then they would be married.

The eldest, Iqbal Chand Khanna, had only recently returned from Cambridge. A proposal had come from Raja Kishan Pershad, the Hindu Prime Minister of the Nizam of Hyderabad. Raja Kishan Pershad claimed descent from Raja Todar Mal, one of the 'nine gems' of Emperor Akbar's court. He was a well-read man who wrote poetry in Urdu and Farsi. He had four Muslim wives and three Hindu wives and he had a total of thirty children from them.

One unique and noticeable feature here was that the offspring of the Hindu wives had Hindu names and a Hindu upbringing; while the children of the Muslim wives had Islamic names and strict Muslim upbringing.

Raja Kishan Pershad wanted one of his Hindu daughters to be married to this fine young man, Iqbal Chand Khanna. Along with this proposal, came the official '*firman*' that he was to join the Nizam's service as the IG police – *firman* is an order from the royal office – not a dowry, it may have been a request from the Raja.

The wedding was conducted with all pomp and ceremony and Iqbal was glad to join the state services.

At the time, Nizam Mehboob Ali of Hyderabad was considered one of the richest men in the world. The apocryphal story of the Kohinoor being used as a paper weight, is one of the many attributed to this unique ruler who believed in nurturing his people and picking the best from the various communities of the country. He brought in the Sikhs to look after the army, while the Anglo Indians were invited to look after and run the Railways. The Parsis came in to run trading houses and the Kayasth Mathurs were brought in for their business acumen. Thus, it was, that, that period of Hyderabad history is known as one of the best.

Be that as it may, within a few years, the other three brothers had also joined the state services of the Nizam of Hyderabad; but they retained their connections with their home city, Lahore.

Meanwhile, at the Malhotra family home, Padmavati had blossomed into a beautiful young teenager. Like all Indian parents everywhere, the Malhotras were a little anxious about the marriage prospects for their first child. The anxiety became palpable especially when they had to attend weddings of other young members of their *dhaighara* clans.

Let me try and clarify this peculiar concept of *dhaighara* (or two and a half houses).

The *Dhaighara* Kshatriyas:

Everyone is aware of the caste system of India – essentially, society was divided into four groups of people, according to the work done by them. The Brahmins were the priests given to learning, teaching and practising the rituals of religion laid down by the Vedas. The next were the Kshatriyas who were the soldiers and warriors – most of the rulers were from this caste. The Vysyas were the ones who dealt with money and finance and trade. The lowest were the Sudras, who largely carried out menial tasks.

This division had its roots in ancient times, thousands of years ago. Over a period of time, many changes had been wrought as the Hindus grew and societal norms evolved. There is enough and more information available on this particular subject.

For the present, we shall deal with the Kshatriyas only. The Kshatriyas or the warrior castes, had three major subdivisions, besides the 52 minor ones. There were the Kapoors, the Malhotras and the top of the pile was reserved for the Khannas. This group was considered the *dhaighara* (of the two and a half houses).

Now, why '*dhai*'?

It appears that 'three' is considered inauspicious, therefore 'two and a half' was okay.

Now, one unique fact about these people was that they 'preferred' to marry within the circle of the *dhaighara*. The catch word here is 'preferred'. Remember, these were business people who had evolved from their warrior identities – after all, if there were no wars, one had to still earn a living – and therefore generate wealth. So, the considerations of land, property and education, besides the history of the families were actually given greater importance than the caste. This was totally the opposite of what the Brahmins practised, for whom caste was always the top priority.

***

It was the *mundan* (scalp shaving) ceremony of the Mehra clan's newest grandson and all the elite business families were going to be present. Jatto and Lajjya Ram were getting ready to attend the grand event together with their daughters Padmavati and Nandrani. They were dressed in glittering silk lehngas with matching kurtis and *odhnis*.

Their heads were not covered – a signal for those who understood such nuances, that these two beautiful girls were unwed, and they were in the marriage market.

Social gatherings like *mundans* and weddings were occasions where eligible grooms and brides were checked out. The wealth and social standing of families were also duly noted.

In one corner, stood a very debonair gentleman with silver grey hair and a briar pipe in his mouth. In a soft undertone Meher Chand Khanna asked the gentleman standing next to him, "Who are these pretty girls? They both look so attractive and…I guess they are sisters!"

"Yes, Khanna Sahib, you are right! They are sisters. They would be a perfect match for at least two of your boys."

"*Nahin yaara*, I must get my elder son Iqbal married first… Anyway, his wedding is almost fixed. He is all set to leave for Hyderabad on the express orders of the Nizam sahib himself. I want him to be married first. But Wazira would be well matched with one of these girls...*kudiyan soni hain...* (the girls are pretty)."

"*Chaliye phir Malhotra nu milke aayiye* (Let us go and meet Malhotra). He will be very happy."

Thus, the ball was set rolling.

Iqbal had already made a name for himself as the IG Police in the state services. The Nizam was pleased with his demeanour and his personality. He had already given his blessings to the nuptials of one of Raja Kishan Pershad's many daughters and this handsome young man. That wedding was solemnized in Hyderabad with all the legendary pomp and show of the state. The *baraat* came on six mounted elephants and many gilded carriages carried the rest of the family to the *Dewan Deorhi*, the fabulous home of the Prime Minister.

One year later, Wazir Chand Khanna was married to Padmavati, the stunningly beautiful daughter of Lajjya Ram and Jatto Rani, the well to do grain merchants of Lahore. After her wedding, Padmavati left Lahore to be with her husband who had also joined the service of the Nizam. Very shortly afterwards, the other two brothers were also invited to join the various services of Hyderabad state.

Two years later Nandrani, the second daughter of Lajjya Ram was married to Trilochan Das Khanna, who came from another wealthy family of grain merchants of Lahore. They were a well-established family, who had for generations been in the business of wholesale grain. The family was originally from Khanna in Punjab. Since Lahore was a bigger and more prosperous city, they had moved in about a 100 years ago.

When both her daughters were married, Jatto found herself pregnant after a gap of ten years. She had had two miscarriages after her two daughters. Luckily for her she carried this child for a full term and in 1928, she had her long-desired son who was fondly named Ram Lubhaya which translates as the favorite of Lord Ram.

Two years later, Nandrani had her first born, a beautiful girl named Swaran. In quick succession she had two more daughters. In fact, when she had her third daughter, the typical busybodies of the *mohalla* came to commiserate with the family.

In stage whispers, one old biddy said to the other,

"Hai hai, teen kudiyan! Inna da ki hovega?" (Three daughters? What will happen to them?)

But the Khanna Matriarch shut them all up by saying, "Don't worry, even if she has three more daughters, we won't come asking you all for help. We can look after our girls."

This then was the leitmotif for the upbringing of the Khanna girls – they grew up with the best of education and an all-round cultural and personal freedom that laid no restrictions on who they could befriend. In fact, the boys also had this very generous and wholesome outlook because no one ever spoke about religious differences, about Hindus and Muslims and about the making of Pakistan.

By the year 1946-'47 they had added three boys and the youngest was barely a year old.

As the dark clouds gathered
Fear and trepidation walked the streets
Leave!
Go Away! Back to your Hindustan!
We don't want you here!

There was fear, there was despair
To leave behind a home so fair
Where will we go? Refugee camp somewhere
Amritsar? Lucknow? Kanpur? Or Delhi?
What will we do? How will we survive?

They had to leave
The girls had to be protected
That little box and its contents too

Yet hope lived on
One more little one and then one died
Rotis had to be made, sabji and dal
Hungry mouths to feed

Hope came
The call from Hyderabad

3

August/September 1947, Koocha Kagaziayaan, Lahore

The embers that had started almost a year ago with the demand of a separate nation were being fanned by Jinnah's cohorts. Hindu families who had been in Lahore for hundreds of years were being told to leave the country...and many did, before all hell broke loose.

***

The days are hazy and the dates are merging into one another. The only overriding thought for the Khanna family is to get to India, as soon as possible. It is a huge decision. There is gloom, there is despair; together with this, a despondent sense of an uncertain future. Well-wishers, friends and family have urged them to get out before they lose their lives. There are three girls, aged 20, 18, and 16 and there are three boys, the youngest, Chetan, is only 20 months old. The maternal grandmother is with them, also fleeing her palatial home. Mrs Nandrani Khanna's only brother, Ram Lubhaya Malhotra is also with them.

The overriding anxiety for the family is to protect the younger generation. The patriarch, Trilochan Das Khanna works for Remington, the typewriter company. He puts the family on a train to Amritsar and goes back to get 'a few more things from the house'. He reaches home and finds it is up in flames. His Muslim dhobi takes him home and keeps him under wraps for a while. He tries to get on a train to Delhi, where the very large refugee camps have been set up. He finally meets up with his family after more than a month.

The train that is supposed to take the Khanna family out from Pakistan has been put on a siding. All of them hide under tarpaulins on a flatbed car. They hear gruesome tales of trains coming from Amritsar loaded with dead bodies and blood dripping all over.

Finally, they board a train for Amritsar (which is the nearest major Indian city) and with great trepidation they pray for safe arrival to India.

The grandmother repeatedly tells Swaran, the eldest daughter, to be careful. Swaran has a small tin trunk with the family jewellery. She also has the responsibility of Chetan, the baby. So, the old lady exhorts her to take care, especially of the jewellery.

Another passenger, a dark swarthy stranger is listening to the exhortations. He understands there is something in that steel box. When the train stops at Jalandhar, where the Khannas are getting off, there are hardly any lights on the platform.

In the dim light, the stranger offers to help them with the box. He grabs it and starts running. The three sisters chase after him; the shouting and screaming brings in help from the others and the box is retrieved.

After spending nearly two years in Delhi, Kanpur and Jalandhar the Trilochan Das Khanna family finally reached Hyderabad. Nandrani's sister Padmavati, who was married in Hyderabad, asked them to come; and helped them set up home all over again – this time for good. They rented a small home and family life started once again.

The boys joined school while the girls joined colleges and life began to swirl around exams, studies, and meals. Their mother, Nandrani, worked hard to provide healthy meals to a growing rambunctious family of boys. The three older girls were a great help and support to their mother. Swaran started taking tuitions, teaching Hindi to the local kids, while the eldest boy Satyen joined work in a bank.

Mr A Venkat Rao, of Marredpally, Secunderabad, was in awe of Mr Trilochan Das Khanna who was a Development Officer with LIC of India, Hyderabad. He admired him for always being immaculately dressed with a tie on, which was just perfect for his role in the LIC. He knew his job well and he identified Rao as a suitable candidate for an agency in the year 1963.

Rao was barely 20 years old and after three years he was selected as the Development Officer. Rao credited his success to Mr T D Khanna and admitted that he tried his best to follow his example while working in LIC Hyderabad.

The Games They Played

In the 1960s, boys and girls had to make their own games and entertainment for themselves. So, while the boys worked out ingenuous strategies, the girls planned new steps for their dance groups, played with the dolls and wooden toys, and all the while they schemed about how they could do all the things their brothers were doing: climbing trees, raiding fruit orchards, teasing the old gardeners with dirty songs and more. The kids did all this, besides playing formally organized games of cricket, softball (what's that?), baseball etc.

A number of girls were fond of playing badminton and there were regular games played at some homes and clubs. In fact, one of the clubs started with just two badminton courts in the open.

Cricket was a great draw even then; and many a young man fancied playing for the state or country. The twin cities had enough role models and the boys enjoyed copying them – how Jaisimha walked, how his collar was always up and never flattened down. All this and more were copied, besides the style of bowling and batting. Regular matches between groups were quite the done thing on a Sunday morning. It is a relief to know that even then, the Parade grounds and Gymkhana grounds were as busy on a Sunday morning as they are today. The open area behind Gita Nursing Home was another favorite spot for scheduled (and unscheduled!) matches!

In fact, Chetan would talk about how, after he had joined the IAF, if he happened to be passing by that way, he would inevitably stop and watch the game.

It may come as a surprise to many, that basketball, softball and baseball were also regular features in Secunderabad. They all seem to have died a natural death. Softball was similar to the American baseball, except for the size of the ball. There were official teams of various schools and they competed against each other. Official tournaments were organized quite regularly.

Every self-respecting boy had a collection of marbles. You could win some, you could lose some, but you could never say that you had 'no marbles at all'. Besides the present-day connotation, meaning you have no brains / gumption, it sort of put you down in the eyes of your peers. A handful of glass marbles were more or less mandatory.

There were two kinds of games that they played with marbles. We have all seen the glass marbles with fancy colourful designs in them, but how many have played with steel marbles? The boys in Marredpally did. The marbles looked like large ball bearings and had quite a weight to them. The rules were more or less the same; although playing with steel marbles must have been rather 'upper crust'!

Hula hoops and stilts were also popular. There were hula hoop races and competitions on the length of time one could rotate the hoop. Races on stilts were also popular and some boys used to get their stilts made to suit their sizes – 'customizing' was not unknown even then! The hoops are less popular now; and one does get to see stilt walkers in the exhibitions sometimes.

Of course, when there were no stilts, there was always the game of '*jharbandar*'! The kids went up on the trees – obviously there were far more trees then! The 'den' had to find and chase them out of the trees! Just think of the exercise that the little legs got! And then there was the innocuous game of 'seven stones'. Seven stones of progressively larger sizes would be placed one on top of the other and the one who could dislodge all of them with one throw of the tennis ball would be the winner.

These were games that were played in a regular kind of way and on an almost daily basis, with teams and groups. There were fights and disagreements, arguments and harsh words. Yet the next day, they were back to jollying each other, comparing notes and sharing confidences. If you fought with a friend, you worked it out so that you got back on an even keel at the earliest.

Marredpally was one of the earliest planned settlements of Secunderabad. There were single bungalows where homes abutted on walls and almost everyone knew who lived where. There were far fewer families although the number of children in each family was far more than what they are today. An average family had four to six kids. They laughed and celebrated together when there was a wedding or any other celebration. They also shared in their pain and suffering equally.

One of the greatest things the elders had was mutual respect. They never interfered in what the children were doing. The fights amongst the kids never went home to the parents and the elders never went to talk to other parents unless it was a very serious matter!

They ensured that the boys and girls went out to play every evening – of course the girls had to be close to the house and the parents had to know where exactly they were playing. Both boys and girls had to be home before the street lights came on!

Kite Flying used to be a passion.

On Sankranti Day in the middle of January, the whole country goes kite flying! At least that is the way it used to be. In the earlier days, there were many more kites in the skies than there are now; And the kites were visible in the skies for many days before the festival and for many days after the festival was over! Needless to say, this was the era before Satellite TV, computers, iPads and what have you, had invaded our lives.

Through the mild winter months of Secunderabad, the boys and some girls, used to be involved in the intricacies of making the very special '*manjha*' – the string coated with very fine glass powder. The one that could cut through all other kites and their strings in such a manner, that the maximum number of kites would come into the kitty of a particular group!

Now we have to remember, that parents and elders were kept out of this particular activity. Old discarded bottles of beer or lemonade would be wheedled out of shops or bars. Then would begin the thrill of smashing them on the rocks – an activity frowned upon – away from adult eyes, and collecting the bits and pieces and pounding the bits further to make really fine powder. Finally, the powder would be strained through a fine cloth. Now the deadly stuff would be mixed with a little jelly from the *kalbanda* (a common cactus plant) and the paste would be applied on the ordinary string. The last part was where the brave hearts would finally deign to wear gloves; otherwise, how would they answer all the questions about bruised and cut fingers and digits? With all this effort, how much of *manjha* did they make? At least 350 yards or nearly a thousand feet – which was also the average length of string that could be rolled on a *chakri!*

Now that the deadly *manjha* was ready, the team was all set to take on the rest of the world. Kites used to cost very little and everyone would pool in and buy at least a dozen. A good '*chakri'* was an essential because the rest of the white string would have to be rolled on it. The free end would be knotted to the special *manjha* which would be closest to the kite. Before the free end of the *manjha* was attached, there was the *'kanni'* to be tied.

This meant that the experts had to come in – this was the most crucial part as this balanced the kite in such a manner that it flew gracefully. So, a senior would hold the kite bend it, tweak it and then decide where the two matchstick holes should be made. Through these two holes would pass the basic doubled thread and then it would be knotted so that when held up by the knot, the kite floated in a balanced way, without tilting to either side.

A badly tied *'kanni'* could ruin a kite as well as be the reason for the air battle to be lost!

Finally, the kite would be ready to fly. The *chakri* would roll out the string and one person would take the kite a little distance away; and then jump, and push it upwards into the sky. The expert holding on to the other end of the string would tug at it and finally get it airborne. Sometimes, it took a couple of faulty starts before that happened! A big shout would go up when the little bird finally began to fly beautifully in the sky. This was also the time when the little sisters and brothers were allowed to hold the string. Otherwise, they were relegated to only holding the *chakri!*

Now, the enemy kite would be spotted!

Ah we have to get this one! So, he comes in closer and our kite comes closer too, till we have a *'pench'* or a lock – where the *manjha* of the other wraps around ours. Now is the final test! Lots of exhortations and instructions from all the team standing nearby; *"Dheel de!"* (let the string reel out!) "*Kheench*! *Kheench!*" (Pull it in! Pull it in!) till finally *"Woh Kaata!!"* (We got it, we cut it!).

Now the spoils of the war – the enemy kite – has to be collected! All the little ones run off in the approximate direction where one can see the kite slowly drifting downwards. One dry branch of a tree, with many prongs on it, is collected and then all the efforts are focused on getting the enemy kite home!

It is obvious that that 'bird' too has to be handled carefully so that it can fly again another day!

5

May 1971

Jinnah's dream of East and West Pakistan fell apart within 25 years of the creating of it. The tall, loud warrior Muslims of West Pakistan could never imagine that these dark-skinned Bengali Muslims of the East could ever disobey their diktat and want freedom for their land. The West forgot that the East took pride in its cultural heritage, its music and its intellectual superiority, notwithstanding its immense pride in the spoken and written Bengali language.

The 1970 elections in the East gave rise to the Bengali nationalist movement and the desire for self-determination. They wanted their own Prime Minister and declared Sheikh Mujibur Rehman as the PM designate. The military junta of the West, could not bear this 'insubordination'.

Operation Searchlight was launched against the people of East Pakistan on the night of 25 March 1971. Very systematically, a mass genocide began and nationalist Bengali civilians, students, intelligentsia, religious minorities and armed personnel, were eliminated. The military junta annulled the results of the 1970 elections and arrested Sheikh Mujibur Rahman.

Members of the Pakistani military and supporting militias engaged in mass murder, deportation and genocidal rape. The capital, Dacca, was the scene of numerous massacres, including Operation Searchlight and the Dacca University

Massacre. An estimated 10 million Bengali refugees fled to neighbouring India, while 30 million were internally displaced. [*Wikipedia*]

India joined the war on 3 December 1971, after Pakistan launched preemptive air strikes on North India. The subsequent Indo-Pakistan War witnessed engagements on two war fronts. With air supremacy achieved in the Eastern theatre and the rapid advance of the Allied Forces of Bangladesh and India, Pakistan surrendered in Dacca on 16 December 1971.

The war ended on 16 December 1971 after West Pakistan surrendered.

***

6

The Three Faujis – With Tales To Tell

Of the five Khanna boys, three joined the armed forces at three different times. As luck would have it the 1971war brought them all into effect in three different arenas. The eldest, Satyen was commissioned as a navigator in the year 1962. The war with China was under way and their passing out parade (POP) was held at Air Force station, Begumpet (then Andhra Pradesh) in a hockey field.

Satyen Dev Khanna spent time in various transport squadrons in Barrackpore, Gauhati and Jorhat. Since he was a navigator, and only transport aircraft had the posts for them, he shuttled between 33 Squadron and 11 Squadron, doing the long-haul flights between the various stations of the East. One of his reminiscences to his son spoke about 'back-to-back ferrying of troops'. For the duration of the 1971 war, he was with No 2 Tactical Air Centre (TAC), where he was actually attached to the Army. 2 TAC was based in Tezpur and was attached to IV Corps which was then commanded by Lt Gen Sagat Singh. I am guessing this is where he was talking about the ferrying of troops because he would have been monitoring troop movements as well as aircraft movement.

During war, as well as during peace time, the TAC acts as a cooperation unit between the Army and the Air Force to achieve a specific or a common goal. It coordinates the two forces to achieve tactical success in destroying a target and making movement of troops and military materials easier. The Tasks of the TAC could include allocation of suitable aircraft and the quantum of weapons in optimum numbers to ensure destruction of the object. The TAC, would at some stage, have total control of the Air operations.

Satyen Dev had very few friends and was known as a very serious kind of guy. One of his good friends was Balu who got in touch with the family after his passing.

Remembering Khannus (Satyen Khanna) by Wing Cdr (Retd) PR Naik (fondly called 'Naikya')

"Oh Yes! It was a bright sunshiny Saturday morning of 9th March, 1963 and the 36 Course mates of 23rd Navigation Course were up early morning, looking ultra-smart – well shaved, with our shining shoes and starched well ironed uniform.

"There was excitement in the air – we were to join the Indian Air Force Officers of the Flying Branch.

"This day saw us "On Top of The World" as we donned our Pilot Officer 'Pips'.

"On Monday, 11th March, we were to depart for our destination with starry eyes looking forward to a super flying career in No 11, Air Force Squadron located at Barrackpore, a historical station.

"Pilot Officers S D Khanna, Balu Shankar Narayanan and I became absolute brothers in arms. A time came when we were called the 'Three Musketeers'.

"Balu and I were a bit *Mastikhore* Twins (fun loving!) but Khannus or Kanni as he was lovingly called was quite sober and mature. He possessed calm, cool, considerate qualities but was very jovial in his typical Hyderabadi style.

"His calm, cool and mature nature stood like a Solid Rock behind us, especially for me.

"One day during my visit to Maharashtra Mandal, Sulabha's mother told me to take the boldest step of meeting her husband.

"She told me that she would fix the time, and to visit them on coming Saturday evening.

"Sulabha's father was a very senior Marchant Navy Officer working as the Harbour Master in Calcutta Port. He was a very tough and strict man. I was shivering in my pants thinking about the forthcoming meet.

"This is the time I knew I could fully lean on my ever cool and mature friend Khannus who was my strongest pillar of support.

"When I spoke to Khannus of my trembling heart full of fear and confusion, he was as cool as a cucumber. With his hand on my shoulder, he told me in his ever soothing but reassuring voice – '*Aare tu mat dar, main hun na tere saath.*'

"His words were worth a million dollars. Till the coming Saturday he kept counseling and guiding me, strategizing what to say and what to avoid.

“On the fixed date, we marched gallantly into Sulabha’s home – No 10, Dumayne Avenue at Kidderpore Dock Road.

“We were greeted by Sulabha's mother who signalled to Khannus ‘All is well’. Khannus just pressed my hand to be calm, cool and collected and that *‘Main Hoon Na’* assurance.

“Sure enough, everything went well with Khannus’ grilling.

“We walked out with broad smiles, bid bye-bye to Sulabha, with Khannus mischievously winking his left eye.

“We walked victorious and with a spring in our steps returned to our rooms in Fort Williams. To celebrate thereafter we went to ‘Nizam’s’ for their sumptuous Kathi Kebab Rolls.

“Sulabha ultimately became my "Ardhangini" and that too on 14th February, 1967.

“At that time, we were not even aware that 14 February is Valentine's Day. What a Coincidence!!!!”

***

Chetan Khanna, known as Chhotu in the Elite Corps of Fighter Pilots was commissioned in 1966 as a Fighter Pilot. After nearly two years of flying training, where he flew Hunters and Vampires for a while, in October1969, he was posted to No 2-Squadron based in Ambala, to fly the indigenous aircraft, the Gnat.

From Wing Commander (Retd) Augustine John Singh ex 2-Squadron, who currently lives in the US, an extract:

“We moved in July-August 1971 to Amritsar for Exercise Operation ‘Cactus Lily’. Johnny Greene (the CO) had convinced us that most wars started with an Exercise, even when Bhutto went to then East Pakistan in October-November 1971 to seek a deal with Mujibur Rehman.

"Sam Manekshaw (the then Army Chief) had promised Indira Gandhi, the then Prime Minister, to deliver Bangladesh once his troops were mobilized and ready. He wanted to do it after the monsoons, when the Northern Passes with China would be closed with snow and ice. Indira Gandhi was determined, and actually wanted Sam to do the job in June.

"After our daily 30-minute run on the taxi track which made our hearts beat a little faster, Greene warned us one day, "Today all of us are standing together. After the war we may not be standing all together."

"He prepared us well as Fighter Pilots flying the little fighter Gnat. He also worked on our psyche; everyday 'God' Greene spoke to us, prepping us up psychologically. When the Pakistani Air Force attacked Rajasansi Airfield, Amritsar on December 03,1971, I clearly remember we were all very excited; but Chhotu had a .303 Rifle in his hands and was jumping up and down outside the 16 ORR and yelling, 'The war has started!' The waiting and the tension were over.

"One day, our Boss man told us, 'In war we will face high speeds, low fuel figures and poor light conditions.'

"Poor visibility and very low fuel during dusk conditions was what Nini Verdi and Patankar faced on December 03, 1971 when the PAF Mirages struck Rajasansi soon after the Signals Unit had been struck by F-104 Starfighters.

"To top it all, Nini Verdi and Pat had to land on a damaged runway!

"As I had only around 50 hours on the Gnat and was not yet Air Defence Operational, I was under the impression that I would be engaged in Base Ops (operations) and other sundry duties.

"I was sitting in the Base Ops with Greene and Jog.

"Greene seeing my sullen face jokingly asked me as to what I was doing there.

"He, with his wicked grin, asked me, 'Don't you want to fly?'

"I replied 'Yes' and nodded.

"He told me to don my G-suit, get my helmet, and get a map. He briefed me to carry out a sector recce all by myself, and not escorted, as hours on aircraft had to be conserved for war. After I had carried out the sortie, he checked me out in the ORP blast pen for a scramble on the Gnat. I met his requirements.

"He then declared me Air Defence Operational. From then on, I was ready to engage the enemy, and carried out ORP duties, strapped up in the cockpit on 2-minute readiness. And while strapped up, I could talk to Maria, my wife, at Ambala through the revived Telemic system by Poonia.

"War started on December 07, 1971; SJ Rana and myself were scrambled for live interception as Mission 69 Alpha & Bravo. I spotted the 2 PAF Mirages heading West and engaged them, and finally got behind one of them at 6 o'clock at 1500 yards with Rana keeping a close eye on the other which had split, having being warned by their radar that two Gnats were behind them. We had only guns. The Gnat had no missiles. I was all set to take a shot with my finger on the trigger. That's it, left high and dry, and the distance started to increase as they were superior aircraft. Gave up the chase and returned to base clearing our Six as they could get after us. I was clocking 600 knots plus, an extremely high speed for a Gnat. One can get into a very unstable condition with slight extra control inputs and kill oneself at that tree-top height.

"I remember Greene calling out for us on R/T, 'Now, Rana, AJ, my boys, take a deep breath, and carry out a Normal Circuit Approach & Landing.'

"He thought it was a trap for us as PAF Interceptors were known to hang around certain areas to intercept our ground attack strike aircraft.

"I remember Chhotu running to the Telly at Rajasansi, donated by a contractor, and stealing a kiss at the newscaster, a pretty Lahori Damsel. I remember him in front of all of us in the evening downing Old Monk XXX touching the screen and kissing his clenched fingers thrice!!! Not once, but thrice! We were waiting to capture Lahore! But the Army had other ideas of avoiding the city totally to avoid the responsibility of logistic problems. We could only see Lahore from the air.

KLPD!!! (*Untranslatable!! Truly no equivalent for this swear word)*

"Yes, your husband and I took part in the 1971 Indo-Pak War from Amritsar. It was fun to have him around.

"Chhotu took part in 'Offensive Sweep Missions' to take on 'Targets of Opportunity' with very strict instructions to not target civilians. The Squadron was on a 'Daytime Air Defence Role', mainly protecting Rajasansi (Amritsar) airfield carrying out Low Level Combat Air Patrol (CAP). God Greene was filled with ideas!

"The people of Amritsar were happy and thankful in many ways to the Squadron for protecting them from damage and casualties. They donated money, a lot of food stuff and other things, woolen textiles and entertained us after the war in their restaurants, clubs and night clubs, repaired our scooters and motorcycles for free, free movies, and even offered their Mistresses.

"I don't know if Chhotu availed of the offer!"

***

The following is from Col JD Khanna (Retd), better known as Akbar. He was commissioned in March 1971.

"My meeting with the First Lady, Mrs Maurine D'silva, even before I joined the Regiment.

"In September, 1971, I was on my way to join the Regiment somewhere in Agartala.

"I had decided to look up my eldest sister in Delhi enroute to Agartala via Calcutta (now Kolkata). I had been instructed by the Adjutant in one of his communications that I was to collect a Putter from the Commanding Officer's Separated Family accommodation while in Delhi.

"I was the newly arrived baby of the regiment and I was to contact the First Lady of the Regiment and seek an appointment to meet her at a time convenient for her. After all, I was being given the privilege of meeting her well before the brother officers of the Regiment. It was an advantage given to very few when the unit is deployed in a field area and one has yet to get on its Rolls.

"I somehow managed to contact Mrs Maurine D'Silva, and having introduced myself, informed her of the task at hand. I was very affectionately invited to dinner by the graceful lady.

"With no experience of dealing with senior ladies, my legs were quaking and I was sweating, standing in front of her door. Finally, I pushed the bell button on her door at the appointed time. A moment later the door opened and there stood Mrs D'Silva, hand extended for me to shake it, welcoming me to her home. She had another gentleman (presumably her brother) there, along with her children. I was offered a seat and told to make myself comfortable and feel at home. Having introduced ourselves with the exchange of pleasantries, the ice was broken and we had a lively conversation. Thereafter, when dinner was laid out, I was really pampered by Mrs D'Silva and she made sure that I stuffed myself silly. I was a little puzzled when she told me that the Officers Mess will make up for this meal once I join up.

"I later realized that as the baby of the unit you sat at the opposite end to the Commanding Officer at the dining table where you were the last to get served and you nearly always got only the leftovers.

"As I was not very familiar with Delhi roads, Mrs D'Silva decided to drop me in her car at a convenient place from where I could manage conveyance back home.

"This wonderful experience left such a mark on my mind that after I got married, I ensured that my wife & I always welcomed the unit bachelors to our home, ensuring they had a full meal, whenever they decided to drop in."

***

Akbar speaks of:

"My initial Days with "Q" (cubic) Battery and my First Shoot as a Gun Position Officer (GPO).

"The Battery (Bty) was composed of Dogras, an excellent fighting clan that believed in 'never say die' and never say that any task was not achievable. My staff in the Command Post consisted of Havildar Kartar Singh Technical Assistant (TA 1), Naik Amin Chand (TA 2), Gunner Shiv Singh (TA 3) and Gunner Pratap TA 4.

"The Signals equipment, mainly C-62 and HM-30 Radio Sets (weighing at least 20 kg each) with two x lead acid Batteries for power (24 volts), were manned by Lance Naik Radio Operator Prem Singh and Gunner Operator Kashmir Singh. My Senior JCO (Junior Commissioned Officer) was Sub Swaran Singh. The Mike NCO (Non-Commissioned Officer) – Signal NCO – was a jovial Havildar Avtar Singh who would make sure that the communication by the EE8 Field Telephone was always available between the OP (Operations Protocol) and the CP (Command Post).

"Came that final day for me to raise the Mega Phone to my mouth and pass on the Fire Orders to the Guns. The Gun Detachments, all set to prove their competence and knowledge of Gunnery, applied all the data passed over to them over the Mega Phone by Second Lieutenant. J D Khanna who was taking his first shoot as the GPO. When the FIRE order was passed to the ranging Gun, the entire Gun end staff including the Sr. JCO would not respond to my orders and I was continuously being ordered by Capt Mahadevan to fire the ranging round.

"I was wondering why the Gun Detachments were not responding, especially the ranging Gun Det (Detachment), when the Sr. JCO told me *'Saab Ji, ek peg rum ka order, fire order se pehele dijiye toh Gun ko Kattichh (pull the firing lever) karega No.3.'* (the firing lever will be pulled only when you order a peg of rum for everyone)!

"I understood that this was the tradition set up by the men to accept a young Officer as their *Maaee Baap* (boss) at the Gun End. My JOY knew NO BOUNDS and I ordered *'Ek Peg RUM sab ke liye'* followed by Fire to the ranging Gun. Later in the day I learnt that this was a set up planned by the Sr. JCO with Capt Kuttan Mahadevan, who in turn enacted the drama as if his OP post was being attacked by the enemy and immediate fire support was required to extricate himself from that place!

***

Another story from Akbar:

The Preparations for 'Op Cactus Lily'

"By end October, early November 1971, it became clear to me, a young soldier, that war was imminent. Preparations had already begun that I was not old enough/senior enough to know, but could see the war clouds hovering overhead. By now Maj Ashok Kumar Sehgal had joined the unit as the new Bty Commander of 592 Field Bty.

"We were briefed by the CO every day on the events taking place and finally after Pakistan decided to preempt and strike our major cities on the night of 01/02 December 1971 we were already deployed for the retaliatory offensive on East Pakistan. What followed is known to all.

"Well, within two days, the airspace over East Pakistan was opened up to our civil air flights. Our Air Force Pilots with their Gnats had taken on the mighty Sabres of Pakistan Air Force. This had ensured us a cut in flying time to just 45 minutes to reach Calcutta as against the 4 ½ hours that I had to bear when I joined the Regiment.

"On the night of 02/03 Dec 1971 we struck out from Agartala and moved towards Akhoura. In two days, we were at Akhoura and then came Brahmanbaria. At Brahmanbaria it was decided that one troop of guns be deployed on the banks of the Meghna River to support the Infantry in establishing a crossing point. I was the one nominated by the CO to lead this Troop of Guns on an independent axis to support our fast-advancing Infantry.

"Not really knowing the terrain and the tracks/motorable roads available to us, Maj. Sriram Dhinkar Kale, the 2I/C, and I decided to drive up the track shown on the map in his Jonga Patrol Vehicle driven by his allotted Driver to recce the route. This was to the west of the road from Brahmanbaria to Bairab Bazaar. We were headed for a place called Bayek on the banks of the river. We moved along the Railway Line for some distance and came across a brick lined track built on an elevated Bundh. We steered left onto the track which could barely accommodate the Jonga wheels.

"However, we must have driven just about a kilometre when we come to a sudden halt and saw that the brick lined road ended there and beyond that was a rickshaw (Passenger Tricycle) track just about 6 feet wide and there were bridges across nalas and streams barely wide enough to let one rickshaw pass over it. We were still on the elevated bandh with no space to turn around. This is where the drama unfolds.

"Our Jonga driver wanted to drive back in reverse gear to extricate the vehicle and us. But how? So, the Driver was being guided by Maj Kale from behind and me from the front of the vehicle – *'thoda left kato, peechhe badho, halt, thoda age lo, ab peechhe chalo...arre bhai steering seedhe rakho, kya kar rahe ho, Samajh mein nahin aata kya?'*

"This carried on for more than an hour and we had barely covered half the distance we were to travel, when suddenly enemy small arms fire opened up from our right. Maj Kale asked his driver if he had drawn the 2I/C's weapon before proceeding for the recce. He said, *'Nahin Saab, aapne bataya hi nahin.'* Next, I was asked if I was carrying my weapon. I sheepishly told him 'No Sir.'

"He then turned to the driver and asked him *'tumhara hathiyar kahan hai,'* you can guess the reply.

"I didn't know whether to laugh or cry at this precarious situation.

"Imagine the three of us in enemy territory in the midst of heavy artillery and small arms fire without weapons for self-defence, trying to extricate a Jonga by driving in reverse gear on top of a bundh where a mere miss would send the vehicle and the driver tumbling down like Jack and Jill about 40 feet below on a nearly dark night.

"We finally managed to get back to the Rail-Track Junction and by early morning were back in the unit Gun Area. Both decided to forget the incident and planned to man handle the Guns from the Rail-Track Junction to the Gun area. The Gun towing vehicles were to be left at the junction only. The execution of this mammoth exercise will be an episode by itself."

***

Some more from Akbar:

Deployment of One Troop of Guns at Bayek -

"We left in the evening to deploy in the hours of darkness. The guns were towed, vehicles loaded as per load tables, including on weapon scale ammunition. We reached the Rail Track Junction in about half an hour's time. The vehicles were dispersed after unloading them and then started the task of pulling the guns physically with drag ropes onto the track to Bayek. Imagine the task of man handling the guns and also hauling the Ammunition and other stores not forgetting rations and K Oil. We were to deploy 16 Kms away from the Rail Track Junction.

"The Guns had to be dismantled to be carried across the rickshaw bridges en-route and re-assembled at the other end. We did this exercise across many such bridges up to the Gun area. We were joined by many civilians from nearby villages in our journey; they were more than willing to assist in carrying our loads. The Guns were deployed well before day break and ready report given to the OP officer Capt J C Sharma and the Adjutant. After breakfast, reduced Detachments were retained to man the Guns and the Command Post and the rest were sent back to fetch the balance of ammunition, other stores such as secondary batteries, rations etc.

"By evening we were well entrenched in our dug-outs though the Guns were never silent since the ready report had been given.

"I take pride in saying that this troop of 3 Guns was supporting an Infantry Battalion across the River Meghna without a break. The Dogras were shuttling up and down to replenish ammunition from the place where the rest of the Regiment was deployed. Hats off to their grit and determination!

"The troop continued to support the Operations at Bairab Bazaar, while the rest of the Regiment was Heli-lifted across the River Meghna. My troop of Guns continued to be deployed at Bayek for next few days. The Paki Guns would open up every night in counter bombardment roll and miss us by miles. I got so used to the Paki shelling, that from the second night onwards, after two drinks and dinner I could sleep like a log."

7

Who am I?

30 Oct 2014, Delhi

I am in Jorbagh in the refugee colony in South Delhi named after Batukeshwar Dutt, the young Indian revolutionary friend of Bhagat Singh.

Swaran still has the box although the jewels are long gone – they paid for the upkeep of the family for the nearly two years they spent in Patiala, Delhi and Lucknow before they finally came to settle in Hyderabad. A few pieces helped the kids marry and settle down. The elders lived out the rest of their lives in rented accommodation.

Swaran married Santosh Kumar Gurtu, a Kashmiri Pandit whose forefathers were eminent journalists and had founded a couple of newspapers in Lahore. He applied for and got this two-room tenement in Jorbagh while the Khannas settled in Hyderabad and opted out of getting compensation for their place in Lahore. It required many trips to government offices which was a little too much for the senior Khanna to manage. His meager earnings from his job were just about enough to keep body and soul together.

Santosh Kumar pulls out a little box and out of it come two watches – a gold chronometer which his father wore and a tiny diamond encrusted watch which was worn by his mother. These are the only two things he was able to save from his burning home. Then he takes me to his daughter Vibha's home where one wall has eight original Kashmir School of Art miniatures done by one of the Gurtu ancestors.

Apparently, this student of History could not let these treasures burn along with his ancient home.

***

04 Nov 2014 Hyderabad

I am back in Hyderabad. Last Sunday, i.e., the 02 November, there was a bomb blast at the Wagah Attari border. Some 60 odd people died on the Pakistani side. Fortunately, the explosion took place in the car park which is quite a distance away from where people sit and watch the show. Any closer and the casualties would have been far greater!

I have to confess – these stories are all true as I was married to Chetan, yes, the baby, who grew up to be a Fighter Pilot in the Indian Air Force. My very affectionate parents in law died within a year of my marriage, barely nudging into their 60s.

Of the 8 children (two were added after settling down in Hyderabad), only 2 survive. From my experience I would like to believe that it was the trauma of uprooting that affected their hearts – and I am not talking in a romantic sense. Ongoing research shows that my suspicions are quite likely true.

EPILOGUE

The two elderly silver haired ladies, Tutu and Lata, were sitting under a sun umbrella on the rolling lawns of the Club. The men folk were talking shop since both of them were from the Army. As they left to refresh their drinks at the bar, the two sisters started speaking.

"I'm surprised Chhutka chose to settle here, after all he has no one here. I wonder why Boudi did not come today?"

"I guess she has her circle of friends and is meeting some of them. I often wonder what happened to Khoka da? Let's ask his brother – he should be able to tell us, especially now that he is here!"

"Before he comes back, let me just check with you, did the rogue ever try his tricks with you after I left?"

"Yes, he tried kissing me; it was a reaction to Ma's telling him if I could be persuaded to drop the idea of marrying my husband."

When the 'boys' got back from the bar, Tutu asked, "*Acchha Chhutka, tor dada kothaye re? (little one where is your elder brother?)*

"Oh! You guys don't know? He died about 15 years ago!"

The sisters looked shocked!

"Of what?"

"Cirrhosis of the liver."

"Did he ever get married?"

"Yes, Ma insisted that he should – although I personally felt that they were destroying that poor girl's life."

"Why?"

"He had not been able to hold on to any job for any length of time. On Baba's request the Municipal Corporation gave him the job of a sanitary inspector."

"What?" There was gasp of disbelief. "Sanitary inspector? With his IIT degree? And his brilliant mind?"

"Yes, alcohol destroyed him completely. His wife left him, essentially to save herself. Then one day we were told to come and collect him; he had to be pulled out of the gutter."

"Was Mesho still alive to see this ignominy?"

"Na, Baba had passed away shortly after Dada's wedding."

"And Mashi? It must have completely broken her?"

"Yes, she developed hypertension and later she had to undergo a bypass surgery. She was with me these last few years. She passed away last year."

"Yes, these last few years have taken a toll on our parents. Ma passed away on the operating table. Ironic. She did not want to be operated for her cataracts in Meerut. She believed Dr Chandra would kill her. So, I took her to Delhi and she died on the operating table. Destiny? karma?

"Baba survived a few more years, he did not know how to live without Ma. He came to stay with me in Jodhpur and he loved the place and our lifestyle. He was all nattily dressed for our New Year party which the Signals Unit was holding in our home. He enjoyed the conversations and the merry making.

"No 35 squadron which Chhotu had commanded in Bareilly, was passing through Jodhpur enroute to Jamnagar… and we got bounced! The whole squadron came to give us a surprise visit! Another friend from the Army was also with us and he was shocked and awestruck at the camaraderie and affection. In a whisper he told Baba that such a thing never happens in the army!

"The next day Baba told Chhotu, 'You know, if I had another daughter, I would marry her in the Air Force.'

"Chhotu winked at me!

"Short of his 90th birthday, we had to wind up house because our posting orders had come. So, Bob, my son, had the onerous job of escorting his grandfather to Delhi where Didi would take over care for him. He did not last beyond his 90th.

"The Meerut house was sold and that was the end of the Meerut saga."

THE CONTINUUM……

Of the five boys and three girls of the Khanna clan, only two are alive. They are well and thriving in Hyderabad.

The Banerji offspring have done better; of the eight girls and two boys, the eldest and the fifth girl have passed on. Four of the sisters have lost their spouses.

The next generation of the Banerji and Khanna clans are all over the world doing well for themselves. Many have married out of the strict confines of caste, creed and religion.

Thank you Kadambini and Nandrani for giving the families such a large and variegated canvas to paint their pictures of life.

You two met each other very briefly but you never knew what imprints you left on the impressionable minds you nurtured.

Thus Life Goes On......

www.ingramcontent.com/pod-product-compliance
Ingram Content Group UK Ltd.
Pitfield, Milton Keynes, MK11 3LW, UK
UKHW042016190726
13854UKWH00005B/2310

9 788194 978244